THE
BEST DARN
SECRET

Susie

Thanks & enjoy!

Linda Hudson Hoagland

THE
BEST DARN
SECRET

LITTLE CREEK BOOKS
A division of Jan-Carol Publishing, Inc.
Johnson City, TN

LITTLE CREEK BOOKS
A division of Jan-Carol Publishing, Inc.

THE BEST DARN SECRET

LINDA HUDSON HOAGLAND

Published October 2012

ISBN: 978-1-939289-00-1
Library of Congress Control Number: 2012918156

You may contact the publisher at:
Jan-Carol Publishing, Inc.
PO Box 701 Johnson City, TN 37605
E-mail: publisher@jancarolpublishing.com

A Letter from the Author

Dear Reader,

I have been a long time and proud resident of Southwest Virginia and the Appalachian Mountains in my small Town of Tazewell. I am a retired employee of the Tazewell County Public Schools where I worked as a purchase order clerk for more than 20 years. I have two sons, Mike and Matt, who are wonderful, of course, a significant other for Mike named Donna and a daughter-in-law, Becky who is married to Matt.

I have been writing all of my, life but I didn't get my first book published until 2006 at the age of 56, and I have been trying to make up for lost time since that date, because I waited so very long to get it done.

I would like to welcome you to my world of the young adult novel with this my first contribution being, *The Best Darn Secret*. What makes this novel unique is that I wrote it when I was a young adult.

Travel with me into the life of Annette Taylor/Ann Patterson to see how she uncovers her past that was taken from her as the result of a car accident that killed her mother and father. When someone tries to kill her, she has no idea why. Follow her steps to the revelation of who she is.

I hope you enjoy *The Best Darn Secret* written when I was sixteen-years-old back in 1965. Technology may have changed, but, the hope of a young girl for a happy life remains a universal dream.

Yours truly,

Linda Hudson Hoagland, Author

Acknowledgments

Thank you to Jan-Carol Publishing and Little Creek Books for allowing me to expand my horizons and move into the young adult field. Janie, Tammy, Sloane and Tara are the ladies with whom I have developed a kinship as they direct me to the correct phrases and thoughts.

Thank you to the readers past and present who take a chance on my words by purchasing a copy to read.

This book is dedicated to the readers

who take a chance on me

and my words.

CHAPTER 1

"Goodbye," said the workers at the movie set. "Have a nice time and a good trip."

Rita waved at the well-wishers until they faded from her vision.

"Isn't it wonderful, Bill?" she said as she moved closer to her husband. "We're finally getting our much needed vacation. We can even take Annette with us and enjoy the company of our daughter. It's been so long since we've spent any time together as a family. It was around this time last year, wasn't it?"

"I believe it was," answered the tanned, fit and handsome man as he drove sitting next to Rita on the front seat of the car.

Rita Taylor was an actress as well as a singer and dancer. Hailed as one of the 1960s most beautiful women, Rita was a statuesque woman with long red hair and blue eyes who didn't like being so famous. She professed her dream of being a plain, ordinary housewife, which was something she knew she could never be, not any more. She liked the good life that being a star had bestowed upon her.

She was older than what most people thought because she had a sixteen-year-old daughter. Rita didn't tell anybody about Annette because she knew reporters from fan magazines would harass her daughter. Neither the daughter nor her parents wanted that kind of treatment. At least, that was the reason Rita repeated over and

1

over to herself. She didn't want to think that vanity about her age was the real reason for not disclosing the existence of her daughter.

Rita had been making a movie in western Tennessee, but Annette wasn't very far away. She and Bill would pick up Annette, and they would be on their way to Virginia for a vacation in the country where they would have time to share with each other as an ordinary family of three. They hoped.

"Now," said Rita to her husband. "Let's hope a reporter from a fan magazine doesn't follow us."

"If one does, I'll lose him or her, or whatever. I won't let any of those fools spoil our plans," said Bill as he glanced in the rear view mirror.

They spent an hour driving around in circles to make sure that no one was following them. When they decided the time was right, they moved on their way to pick up Annette.

Rita was disguised because she wanted no one to recognize her. She had on a brown wig and wore blue jeans and a sweatshirt.

Bill didn't need to wear a disguise. All he had to do was remove his toupee. He had a receding hairline, and he didn't look like the same man without the purchased hairpiece.

Annette was living at the Sunnydale Orphanage. She said she really didn't mind it too much because she had been living at Sunnydale for such a long time that it was home to her. She could not remember living with her parents at any time, and she doubted that she had ever lived with them. She only vacationed with them whenever it was convenient.

The people running the orphanage were very happy with Annette's presence in their facility because the Taylors donated large sums of money to help out with all of the expenses of running the place.

Annette was treated as an ordinary child. She wasn't supposed to tell anyone about her parents, and she didn't. Many times she longed to shout it out from the rooftops that her mother was Rita

2

Taylor, the actress, but she didn't. She did her best to honor their request for secrecy.

Whenever her parents took her places, she told the other children, when they asked, that they were people who wanted to adopt her. She didn't like to lie, but what else could she do?

She had to sneak her clothes out without letting anyone see her do it because she didn't want anyone to see her two suitcases. It would be hard to explain to the orphans about why she was allowed to stay with prospective adoptive parents for two weeks. She knew if she was spotted, there would be plenty of questions.

An old car drove up to the front of the building, and she knew immediately that it was her parents. They weren't driving the Cadillac. Instead, they were driving an older model car, probably for privacy purposes she guessed. They didn't want to be recognized. Annette hoped it was because of the fear that they might be bothered by Rita's aggressive fans.

Most of the other children were eating lunch and hopefully wouldn't notice the car or the visitors.

Rita and Bill went inside the office building to talk to the supervisor, Mary Boothe.

Annette knew it was her cue to start the ball rolling. She picked up both suitcases and walked down the deserted hall. She had to go down two flights of stairs. Whenever she saw someone coming, she would set the suitcases in rooms with open doors so they wouldn't be seen. She acted as if she was casually walking along the hallway on an errand.

She arrived at the front door where she looked around to see if anyone was outside. She saw no one, so she picked up one of the suitcases and started walking. She was almost to the car when she was spotted by Nina, her best friend in the entire world. Nina was a pretty girl with short blonde hair and beautiful blue eyes.

"What are you doing?" asked Nina. "Did someone adopt you?"

"No," replied a worried Annette. "I wasn't adopted, and I'm just helping some lady carry her luggage to the car."

"Why would a lady be moving out of the orphanage when it's only for kids?" Nina probed.

Annette knew she was trapped.

"Nina, I'll tell you the truth if you promise not to breathe a word of it to anyone," said Annette in an excited whisper.

"Cross my heart, hope to die," said Nina as she made the sign of a cross over her chest.

"I'm going on vacation with my mother and father."

"Your mother and father? I thought you were an orphan, just like me," said Nina.

"Well, I'm not. Rita Taylor, the actress, is my mother."

"You're kidding?"

"No, I'm not," said Annette.

"I thought I was your best friend, Annette. Why didn't you tell me about this sooner?" asked Nina with a voice tinged with hurt.

"I couldn't. Mom didn't want me to tell anybody."

"Why live in an orphanage?" asked Nina.

"Why not?" answered Annette.

"I could think of a lot of reasons why not," replied Nina. "Number one would be that you would have your own parents and your own place to live with your parents. You would have your own room and your own spending money. You wouldn't be forced to accept hand-me-down clothes and have to share everything you value with other kids who don't know how to take care of anything. Those reasons are just for openers. Do you want me to go on?"

"No, Nina. It's just better this way, and I have always liked living here. It's like I have two families. My mother and father are really a vacation family; a make-believe family that I get to see once in a while. On the other hand, you are like a sister to me. You and everyone here in this place are my family."

"I really don't understand this whole thing," said Nina.

"Sometimes I don't understand it either. You won't tell anyone about it, will you?" asked Annette.

"No, I won't. They wouldn't believe my anyway. I'm not sure I believe it myself," replied Nina.

"I wouldn't lie to you. You're my best friend."

Annette carried the first suitcase to the car, and Nina offered to help with the second suitcase. Annette gladly accepted the help.

When Rita and Bill exited the building, they saw Nina. Annette could tell from the look on their faces that they didn't like having another person know about their secret.

"She won't say anything to anybody. She gave me her word, Mom, Dad."

"I hope not," said an irritated Rita.

"I trust her. You guys can, too."

"I won't tell a soul about you. It's such a pleasure to meet you, Miss Taylor. Would it be possible to get an autograph from you?" asked Nina.

Rita became even more agitated by Nina's request for an autograph.

"If I give it to you, how will you explain it to the other children?"

"I won't. I'll hide it away where it won't be found so I can keep it forever," gushed Nina.

Rita reached into her handbag and located a small notebook. She signed a piece of paper, ripped it from the notebook and handed it to Nina.

"Don't tell anyone," admonished Rita as she turned to climb into the car.

"I won't, I promise. Have a wonderful vacation, and Annette, please write me."

"I will as soon as I can," whispered an excited Annette as she squirmed in the back seat of the car trying to make herself comfortable.

When the car pulled away from the curb, the cheerful wave and happy smile disappeared from Nina's face. She was worried because she had a feeling something would go terribly wrong. She hoped that Annette returned to the orphanage at the end of the two weeks as she had planned. She wanted to see her best friend again before she, Nina, celebrated her birthday. Nina was seventeen and would be eighteen years old next month. That meant she would have to leave the orphanage, which was fine with her, but she wanted to remain in touch with Annette forever.

CHAPTER 2

Rita, Bill and Annette were very happy because they were all going to be together. The only thing on their daily agenda was fun; no early wake up calls, no grumpy coworkers and no life or death decisions to be made.

The wig Rita wore was very becoming, but Annette didn't like it. She helped her mother take it off her head. She stared with envy at her mother's long red hair.

"Gee," she sighed. "I wish I had hair like yours, Mom."

"What's wrong with your hair?" Rita asked. "I think it's very pretty."

"Oh, it's such a mousy color," Annette answered. "It's just plain mousy brown."

Rita interrupted her by saying, "How would you like it if I lightened it a little? Just a little, mind you. I have to admit, it is a dull color."

They had been driving for quite a while when Annette exclaimed after a yawn, "I'm hungry."

"So am I," added Rita. "Why don't we eat at the next drive-in restaurant? Is that all right with you, Bill?"

"All right with me," replied Bill as he tried to hide a yawn.

They kept driving and driving until they finally found place to eat. They were so few and far between on the rural route they were traveling, they thought they would never find one.

What they did see was miles and miles of rolling hills where the forests had given way to the grazing cattle in shades of brown, black and white. Those rolling hillsides led to the purple majestic mountains that surrounded them.

"Finding a place to eat is like looking for hen's teeth. Of course, hens don't have teeth," Annette said as she laughed at her own joke and continued to laugh until tears rolled down her cheeks.

"Where did you hear that?" asked Rita while laughing with her daughter.

"I don't know. I probably heard one of the new kids from the country say it. It was so pitiful. Harry, that's the boy, said his parents were killed in a fire. They had no place to go, so they had to come to the orphanage. Harry, his brother and two sisters are going to be separated because a family wants to adopt the two younger kids. I don't think they should separate them, do you?"

"I don't know, dear," said Rita. "Maybe they have to separate them. That's the only way they will get to live like real kids with real parents. Anyway, it would be one chance in a million that a family would want to adopt all four kids."

"But I still don't think they should be separated," said Annette.

"Your mother's right. I doubt if they could ever find a family that would want all four children," said Bill.

"Mom, will I ever be able to live with you and Dad like a real kid with a real family?" asked a solemn Annette.

"Of course you will, honey, and soon I hope," answered her father as he forced a big smile on his face and glanced in the rearview mirror.

"When is soon?" asked Annette.

"As soon as they stop calling me to make movies," said an angry Rita. "Women age out of stardom really quickly because the cameras can't be fooled. It really shouldn't be much longer, whether I want to quit or not. They don't write good roles for an aging female star. We don't even get a chance to fade away. We just disappear."

"Here comes our food," said Annette staring at the tray as it was attached to the side of the car by the teenage waitress. "I'm starved."

"Dad, please turn on the radio," Annette said.

Annette was enjoying the music, and when the commercials came on, she didn't mind them either. She especially enjoyed the one about driver's training.

"Dad," she said softly. "Will you teach me to drive?"

"He certainly will not. I don't want my daughter driving all over creation. You would probably speed all the time," answered Rita in Bill's place.

"You know how to drive. Why can't I learn how?" questioned Annette.

"Yeah, why can't she?" queried Bill as he joined the conversation. "I could teach her, and she already knows the fundamentals."

"Where did you learn them?" asked Rita as she stared into her daughter's eyes.

"Dad taught me whenever you weren't around. He knew you would object. Anyway, I'm old enough to get a license," she said hoping her mother would say yes.

"I guess I'm outnumbered; two against one. You and your father are both against me," said Rita with a worried look on her face.

"Oh, thanks, Mom," said Annette as she leaned forward and kissed her mother on the cheek.

Bill stopped the car, and Annette climbed into the driver's seat. She was so excited and wanted so much to impress her mother.

She started the motor and sat for a little while until her father urged her to move. She moved the gearshift to drive and stepped on the gas pedal. Now she would have to steer. They were on level land, and if she couldn't steer correctly, the worst she could do was run into a ditch, which was exactly what she did, but she drove out of it without any problem or damage to the car.

"How am I doing, Dad?" she asked, hoping to hear nice words.

"Great, you're doing just fine," he answered. "Almost as good as me."

She looked in the rear view mirror at her mother but didn't say anything. She knew her mother didn't want her to drive, but she was having so much fun she didn't want to stop.

She drove about two hours before she got tired. She asked her father if he would trade places. He turned around and asked Rita if she would like to move back to the front seat indicating that the driving lesson would soon be ended. Rita consented gladly, because she was afraid of being in the same car with Annette driving. The fact that she was clinging to the car door with her knuckles white from strain proved her point.

They drove for several hours, and it was getting dark. Rita suggested that they rent a room at a motel.

They had made several unplanned stops along the route sightseeing at the overlooks that spread the beauty of the mountains before them like a living portrait and generally snooping at yard sales and flea markets which delayed their arrival. Bill continued to drive until it was completely dark before they stopped. They were trying to reach their destination before stopping for the night, but they were too tired to continue. Rita was cross and tired. She complained about everything.

"It's too hot in here," said Rita.

"Turn on the air conditioner, Mom," replied Annette.

"I'm going to take a shower," said Rita.

"Okay, I'm going to watch television. Dad's gone to get something to drink."

"The water is too cold. I can't get it adjusted right," Rita shouted angrily.

"You want me to do it?"

"No, no, never mind," Rita mumbled.

She was still cross when they were going to bed. Bill tried to kiss her good night, but she just turned her head and went to sleep.

The next morning, Rita's mood had not improved.

"Mom, have I done something wrong that has upset you so much?" asked a concerned Annette.

"No, it has nothing to do with you," answered Rita.

"Then what is it? Is there anything I can do or say that will make it better?"

Rita knew she was going to have to explain the whole mess to her nearly grown-up daughter. Rita reached for a tissue and bit her lower lip as she tried to stem the tide of tears.

"I'm going to have a baby," she said. "And I don't think your father wants another child."

"What?" Annette cried.

"Oh, I don't know. He just seems against any more children," said Rita sobbing.

"Are you going to tell Dad, now?" asked Annette. "I think you should. He ought to know."

"I'll tell him, but not until I know how to," said Rita. "And I hope he forgives me."

"Forgive you? I think it's wonderful!" exclaimed Bill.

"You were eavesdropping," snapped Rita.

"Of course I was. I was in the bathroom, and you know these walls are like paper," said Bill with a huge grin.

"You're not angry? You want to have a baby, even at our age?"

"Sure, honey," he said as he embraced his wife softly.

"I'm so happy!" said Rita throwing her arms around her husband's neck.

"So am I," he replied. "So am I."

"It will be nice to tell the world that I'm going to have a baby. Just think, Bill, our own little bundle of joy."

Annette looked at them with all kinds of hurt feelings etched into her young face.

"What am I? An orphan? Is that why I have to live at Sunnydale?" she asked as she fought back the swelling tide of tears.

"No, no, Honey, you're our secret. You are the best darn secret we've ever had," said Bill as he hugged his daughter who was displaying obvious signs of dejection.

It didn't take them long to finish dressing and continue their trip. They didn't eat at the motel because none of them were hungry. They decided to wait until they found a restaurant.

When they finally decided to eat, it was already noon. They stopped at a small roadside café where they ordered a skimpy lunch and continued with their trip. They all had different reasons for the lack of appetites. Rita was suffering from morning sickness. Bill was too excited and happy to care about food. Annette was lonely and left out once again.

"Dad, let met drive for a while," said Annette.

"I don't think so, not today," he answered.

"Why not?"

"Your mother isn't comfortable with you behind the wheel."

Annette accepted that explanation for a short while until she worked up the nerve to ask again.

"Mom, tell Dad it's okay to let me drive. I'll never be able to drive unless you guys let me practice."

"Annette, your father said no," snapped an irritated Rita.

"Dad only said no because of you. You're the one who is afraid, Mom. How come you're so afraid of letting me drive?"

"Annette, please give it a rest. I'm not afraid of letting you drive. I just think a more experienced driver needs to navigate some of these country roads."

"She really drives well, Rita," said Bill. "I think we should let her get in some practice. I'll take over when the roads get more dangerous if I think she can't handle them."

"Thanks, Dad," said Annette as she smiled at her mother. With her father's help, she knew she had won that battle.

Annette was driving very well. They were going up and down mountain roads with ease, but she didn't like some of the sharp curves because they gave her the jitters.

She was going up an exceptionally steep part of the mountain. As she crested the highest point and was starting to go downhill again, she pushed the brake pedal. She pushed her foot to the floor again and again with no slowing of the car whatsoever.

Her father noticed the scared look on her face and the excessive speed they were traveling.

"What's wrong?" asked Bill as calmly as he could.

"The brakes are gone!" screamed Annette.

"Pull the emergency brake!"

She yanked and yanked, but it was stuck.

"Let me do it!"

"Bill, what's wrong?" asked Rita.

Bill leaned toward Annette and struggled with the lever positioned between them. He neither acknowledged Rita's question nor did he attempt to answer her.

"Oh, God, I knew it was a mistake to let her drive the car. We're all going to die!" screamed Rita.

"Not if I can help it! Don't blame Annette for this. We don't have any brakes, and that's not her fault!" shouted Bill.

Annette steered while her father pulled at the emergency brake. She released her seat belt and scooted over closer to the door so he would have some extra working space.

They were now going up another hill that slowed them down a bit, but they still didn't stop. They approached the top when her father raised his head which bumped Annette's arm forcing her to release the steering wheel, which caused her to lose control. Her father was almost horizontal as he tried to pull the emergency brake again.

When she crested the top of the hill and the car went off the side of the road, the door flew open. Annette fell out of the car, but Rita and Bill went down with the car into the deep ravine, narrowly missing the water at the bottom.

The world was black.

Annette seemed to have fallen into a cave filled only with darkness.

She was blindly running and searching for light, any light. She needed a way out of the cave.

Her heart was racing as she became more frightened with each passing moment. Her breathing was rapid, almost like the panting of an animal, a frightened wolf maybe.

She was running, but she couldn't feel anything solid beneath her feet. She was climbing steps, but she couldn't see them or feel them.

Up and up she climbed but still no light; no hope; no help.

She wanted to scream, but she couldn't open her mouth. She couldn't force her vocal chords to create sound.

The dark cave had no sides, no top and no bottom that she could feel. She continued to climb up and up until she faltered as if she had lost her footing and started to slide backward a little. She tried to reach out her hand and stop herself from falling all the way to the bottom.

She couldn't move her hand. She couldn't see her hand.

All of a sudden, she stopped falling backward.

She seemed to right herself and continue climbing. She was retracing her steps climbing up toward . . . what?

There was no light to be seen. No help could be had. Why was she going up and up?

She had to keep going, keep pushing and keep climbing up the stairs she couldn't see, toward a goal she knew nothing about other than a feeling, a notion, that it was the way out to the light that would guide her to safety.

Safety from what? Why was she in this murky, deep, dark, black cave? Why was she climbing a stairway that wasn't there? Why was she searching for a light that had disappeared? Was it gone forever? Would she be climbing these stairs forever?

A flash! What was that? Was it a flash of light? Where did it come from?

There it is again. But, it's gone again. *Why doesn't it stay? she thought. Why doesn't it show me where it is? At what point does it begin?*

Another flash illuminated so bright that it made her duck her head down away from the harsh, lightning fast brilliance.

She didn't close her eyes because she needed to see where the light originates. She needed to go to the light away from the darkness.

She tried to force herself to move faster, but she was slowing down.

The light appeared to change. It was no longer a brilliant instant flash. It became a steady glow that grew as she climbed closer and closer to it.

The glow from the light filled her head and she was released from the clutches of the dark, black cave.

She needed to open her eyes. She forced her eyelids up so she could see into the bright world where she returned to from the dark, black cave.

Annette lay by the side of the road for a while. She heard a loud noise. It was a siren, and it was so shrill that it hurt her head. She opened her eyes so she could see what was causing the noise. It was getting louder and louder until she got up and started running away from the road and away from the sound. She ran until she couldn't hear the siren anymore.

A neighbor saw the car go over side of the road and called the police. He also told them to send an ambulance. He didn't see Annette fall out of the car so he thought there were only two people in the car. The police found only two bodies and assumed there were only two to be found.

CHAPTER 3

Annette scrambled to her feet and ran until she was tired of running. She was so thirsty. She saw a mountain stream and stopped to get a drink of water. The water refreshed her a little, and she washed the cuts and bruises on her legs and arms.

Her head was throbbing with pain. She reached to the back of her head and felt the blood. She washed off as much of the blood as she could with the cold water and tore the bottom from her blouse to make a bandage that she tied into place around her head just like she had seen in her mother's last movie.

She started to get up but fell backward with her face to the sky. She was gone again back into the black, dark cave. She couldn't find any strength to propel herself back up the steps. She couldn't force her feet to move, to climb or to search for the light. She remained on the ground for several hours, enduring the hot blistering sun and the insects.

She didn't have the energy or the will to move except in her dreams. Her mind's eye seemed to focus on her family. She saw her red-headed mother and handsome father with their arms reaching for her. Before they actually touched her, her mother and father disappeared from view as if they were swallowed up by the deep, dark cave from which she had been trying to escape.

"Mommy, Daddy, where are you?" she whimpered like a small child.

She thrashed around in the tall grass that surrounded her body.

"Come back, Mommy, Daddy, please come back!" cried the voice of a young child.

Suddenly she saw a house. Not the mansion her parents occupied but a house with a white picket fence lovingly enclosing the family in its watchful arms; a house like she always dreamed for her mother, father and herself to live and love in.

The white picket fence was only a means of keeping the bad people away from her family. It always permitted the good people to enter and welcomed them as they passed through the gates.

She saw the upstairs windows of the house blinking at her, as if they were eyes much like her own. The window shades were acting as eyelids as they periodically raised and lowered covering the windows.

The entrance to the house was in the shape of a smile. There was a set of double doors beckoning the family to walk through the smile into blissful happiness.

She saw her mother, father and herself walking and talking inside the house. All of them were smiling and happy.

The happy scene lingered ever so long. Suddenly she started seeing signs of deterioration and ruin crawling over the structure and the fence like a great fungus that was growing and spreading its way to cover every bright, happy surface.

The paint on the house blistered, and when the blisters broke, they exposed graying and decaying wood. The window shades no longer went up and down like blinking eyes. They remained open as if they were lifeless and staring into an uncaring world.

The smiling entranceway sagged into an unhappy, unwelcoming frown with the doors slammed shut. The white picket fence faded to gray with many of the pickets broken off and displayed a toothless, lifeless appearance. No one entered the house. No one wanted to walk into something that appeared so menacing and uninviting. There was no happy family shouting "hellos" and waving to passersby. They were all gone.

Annette stood outside the broken fence looking into the ruins of what was once a happy life. She felt the tears flowing down her cheek as she watched her dreams fade into nightmares. She raised her hand to brush at the tears from her dampened cheeks. She moved her arms. She flexed her hands. She was back. Annette was no longer lingering in the holding cell consisting of the dark, black cave waiting for death to overtake her.

She opened her eyes to see a rifle in her face. She tried to pick herself up from the ground, but she couldn't. Her head was hurting, and she began to cry. She couldn't hold the tears back.

"Help me," she said, barely audible.

The young man holding the rifle had walked a good distance from his home. He didn't know what to do with the girl. He was afraid she might die if he left to get somebody to help him carry her. He stuffed his rifle under some brush for safekeeping. He picked her up, hoisted her over his shoulder and started walking toward his home and the help he would need to get her back on her feet again.

He was getting tired as he climbed over the hilly terrain, so he gently laid her on the ground so he could rest for a few moments. It wasn't much further, but he needed a short breather.

He watched her fight to bring herself back from the dark hole of unconsciousness. Her body would jerk and flinch with each struggling step her mind took toward the real world.

She awoke long enough to say, "Don't shoot. Please, don't shoot me."

With her lying on the ground looking so helpless, he didn't know what to say. He surely wasn't going to shoot her. Then he remembered his rifle and how it had been pointed at her.

"I'm not going to shoot you," he said apologetically, but it was in vain because she had passed out again.

He decided to go get his rifle while she was unconscious. Rifles were expensive, and he didn't have enough money to buy another one. His father always told him to carry the shotgun while hunting for small game, but Luke preferred the rifle. He might miss his shot a little more often, but it didn't pepper the meat with small shot. He ran like the wind, so it didn't take him very long to get to his rifle and then return to where he had left her lying on the ground.

She was gone. Where did she go? He was worried, really worried. That poor, sick girl all alone. His house wasn't far from where he was standing. He could go and get his father to help him look for her. She was such a pretty girl. He didn't want anything to happen to her. He wouldn't want anything to happen to her even if she was as ugly as a mud fence.

Luke was a young man of twenty, farm boy handsome, who lived with his father. His mother had died when he was four years old during the birth of his little sister. His grandmother and sister, Emma, lived there, too as one big happy family. They were happy because they weren't missing what they never had. They didn't know they should feel unhappy because they were poor and just barely surviving.

He knew all his friends his age were married, but he had never found a girl he loved enough to marry. Usually one date was enough to let him know he wasn't interested.

"Pa! Pa! Come quick. You've got to help me look for a girl," shouted Luke as he rushed into the house.

Luke's father, Harry Hamilton, came running to see what was wrong. Luke repeated what he said.

"What's the matter son? Can't you look for one by yourself? You know there's plenty in town for you to choose from," Harry answered with a chuckle.

"No, that's not what I mean," Luke said angrily. "Follow me, I'll tell you on the way."

Harry grabbed for his gun.

"You don't need your gun," said Luke.

"Okay, boy, whatever you say."

"Hurry, Pa, please hurry."

Luke kept looking toward the ground and Harry asked, "What are you looking for? Footprints?"

"No, Pa. I'm looking for blood," Luke replied. "She was bleeding all over from cuts. I don't know what caused them either."

They traveled further.

"Pa, look, here's some blood," said Luke pointing toward the ground.

They went from spot to spot. They didn't raise their heads from the ground. They kept following the trail and didn't stop for anything.

"I don't think she's very sick," said Harry. "If she was she couldn't go so far."

"She was sick, real sick. She was afraid that's why she's running," said Luke. "She woke up and saw me pointing a rifle at her. Well, I wasn't really pointing it at her. It was pointed toward the ground, and she was on the ground. Pa, she's sick. She had cuts all over her and a big one on her head. She was burnt all over from the sun. We've got to find her."

Just as soon as he said that, he stopped. There she was lying in the tall weeds near a cluster of trees. Her clothes were partially torn off of her body from running through the brush and briars. Her hair was tangled with thorns, leaves and partially dried blood.

Luke went over to her and picked her up. He placed her across his broad shoulder and started running toward home. Harry followed as fast as he could.

CHAPTER 4

Luke pushed the door open and gently laid her on the sofa.

"Emma, Granny, come help me, please!" he said as he struggled to regain control of his breathing.

"Who is that?" asked Emma as she stood next to Luke staring down at the scratched and bloody body of a young girl.

"I don't know. I found her in the woods."

"Did she say anything?" asked Emma.

"Nothing that would help figure out who she is," replied Luke.

"We'll get her cleaned up. Maybe she'll wake up soon," said Granny as she looked at the stranger.

"Okay, I'll get one of my nightgowns for her. I'll throw a clean sheet across my bed. You can bring her in there so we can get her undressed and patched up."

As soon as Emma had the bed prepared, Luke gently placed his strong arms under the stranger, lifting her from the sofa. He slowly carried her to Emma's bedroom and carefully placed her on the clean white sheet.

"Now get out, boy, so we can help this girl," said Granny as she pushed Luke to the door.

"I wonder who she is," whispered Harry.

"I don't have any idea. All I know is that she needed help," answered Luke.

After the girl was dressed and under the covers, Luke entered the room. He looked down at her and smiled. He hoped she was going to be all right.

They didn't have enough money to call a doctor, so Emma and Granny had to watch her. Because Luke was the one that found her, he felt it would be his responsibility to look after her.

"Don't shoot," she kept mumbling over and over.

"Why does she keep saying that, Luke? Who would want to shoot her?" asked Emma with concern for her patient.

"She thought I was pointing my rifle at her," he said. "All I was doing was holding it pointed toward the ground for safety reasons. She got it in her head that I was going to shoot her."

"She's got cuts all over her, and the gash on her head is pretty deep. What do you think happened to her?" asked Emma as she watched her patient breathe deeply and evenly.

"She looks like she rolled down a hillside. Her cuts and scratches are on the front and back of her body," said Luke.

"I wonder how long she was knocked out? Look at her sunburn. She must have been lying in the sun for hours," said Emma.

"It sure looks that way," agreed Luke.

Annette had a terrible sunburn. Her face was blood red, as were her neck, arms and legs. It was almost like getting a burn from the stove. She couldn't be touched without causing her pain.

Luke saw her eyes open.

She saw him and screamed, "Don't shoot! I'll leave!"

"I'm not going to shoot you. Honest to God, I wouldn't hurt you at all!" he exclaimed.

He reached his hand out to her, and she flinched.

"I won't hurt you. I promise I won't hurt you," he pleaded.

He smiled, and so did she; or at least she tried to smile.

"What's your name? She's Emma and my name is Luke," he said trying to break the ice.

"Uh, my name? Why do you want to know my name?" she asked with a frightened look in her eyes.

"What do you want me to call you? How about Freckle Face, Squint Eyes, Chief Red in the Face, or Little Miss Cut-up?" he replied with a smile.

"Why would you call me those names?" she asked, confused.

"Look in this mirror. Then you'll see why," said Emma as she handed the girl a small looking glass.

Annette glanced at herself momentarily before setting the mirror aside. She did not recognize the face looking back at her.

"What do you think my name is?" she asked.

She didn't know what to tell him. She couldn't say she didn't remember. What would he think? What would he say?

"I'd say your name is Ann. Am I right?" he asked.

Why couldn't she say her name was Ann? That would do for now anyway.

"You're right. My name is Ann. How did you know?" she asked.

"Oh, I just guessed. You look like your name would be Ann," Luke said with a triumphant gleam in his eye.

"I am so tired, and my head hurts. Do you mind leaving the room? Please, don't think I'm rude," she said as she covered her face with her hands.

She had to get rid of him. She had to concentrate and try to remember her name.

Luke went out of the room and told the rest of the family her name was Ann.

Emma was a young lady of sixteen and was the same height and size as Ann. She was in the eleventh grade at school and very popular. She could go on a date every night of the week if she wanted but didn't because some of the boys were too fresh. Some of them drove all the way from town for a date, but she wouldn't go out with them.

If any of the interested young men tried to hurt or bother her, Luke would take care of them. Luke loved his sister very much and didn't want to see her hurt.

Emma had blonde hair and blue eyes, and she was on the short side. She and Luke were obviously brother and sister except Luke was much taller than Emma. She had an appealing look of innocence about her that attracted many second looks from men.

Emma fixed Ann's supper tray and was about to take it to her.

"Emma, can I take the tray in?" Luke asked as he was reaching for the paper.

She handed him the tray and opened the door for him. He set the tray down and closed the door behind him so he could have some privacy.

"Ann," he said gently. "I brought the paper. I thought you might like to read it."

He handed the newspaper to her, and she glanced at the headlines:

ACTRESS RITA TAYLOR
AND HUSBAND KILLED

Beneath the bold headline was a professionally posed photograph of the deceased couple. She laid aside the newspaper and looked at Luke. She had decided earlier that the next time Luke came into the room, she would tell him her problem. He would help her because he had already. Luke seemed really nice. He would help her find out her identity.

"Luke," she said. "There's something I should tell you. You probably won't believe me but listen to me anyway. I told you my name was Ann, didn't I? Well, anyway, it isn't. At least, I don't think my name is Ann. I don't know who I am or where I am or what caused these injuries. I don't know what to say or do. Will you please help me?" she pleaded as tears filled her eyes.

Luke didn't know what to say, but his heart was melting away with a newborn affection for the little lady in distress.

When he finally found the words he asked, "How can I help you?"

"I don't know, but try somehow," she said as she started to cry. "I have to know who I am."

He sat there staring at her before he finally said, "What can I do?"

"Did you find a purse, a wallet or anything that would lead to my identity?" she asked hopefully.

"No," he said with a sigh.

"Don't tell the rest of your family, will you? Let them think my name is Ann. Please try to help me. I'm counting on you. You're the only one I can ask. I have no one else," she said turning her head toward the window.

"I won't tell them for now," Luke agreed.

He knew he would have to tell them eventually. He didn't like keeping secrets. Luke left the room, and Ann fell into a restless sleep.

Luke paced the floor. When his father told him to sit down, he couldn't. He had to think. Was there something where he found her that would tell him who she was?

It was almost bedtime when Ann asked Emma to tell Luke to come in to see her.

Luke walked in and sat on the edge of the bed. Her eyes were closed, so he started to leave.

"Don't leave," she said in a laughing sort of way. "I'm only playing possum."

He laughed with her and walked away from the door.

"Ann, don't you remember anything?"

"I can remember a little," she said with a sigh. "I remember getting up and running because of a loud noise. I remember lying in that hot sun, too weak to move. The burning was terrible, but

26

I couldn't move. Then I remember a gun, a rifle, I think. Well, anyway you were carrying it. I remember water and trying to clean up my cuts and scratches."

"Do you remember what the loud noise was?" he asked hopefully.

"No," she said glancing down at the blankets. "I'm sorry to cause so much trouble. You're the only one I would ask."

"A loud noise. What could that be? You don't have any guesses?"

Ann closed her eyes and answered negatively with a side to side motion of her head.

Luke promised he would help her one more time before he went to his room and climbed into bed. He couldn't sleep. He tossed and turned the whole time he was in bed.

He crawled out of bed and found a book. Maybe if he read a few pages it would make him sleepy. He read half of a chapter, but when he tried to remember what the words had said, he couldn't. All he could think about was Ann.

He pulled on his blue jeans and shirt as he grabbed his shoes and a flashlight and tiptoed out the door. The nearest neighbor was two miles away, so he didn't think he would be bothered by anyone. He hoped no one would think he was a scavenging bear and take a shot at him. He was going to look for a clue.

Luke first went to the place where he found her the second time. There was nothing there. He used the flashlight as he scratched around in the weeds looking for evidence.

He retraced his trail and went to the place he first saw her. He looked and looked. He pulled at the weeds that had been mashed to the ground with the weight of her body. He found spots of blood and some torn fabric, perhaps a makeshift bandage she had torn from the shirt she had been wearing.

He walked near the stream and saw where she said she had tried to wash her cuts and scrapes. He was about to leave when he shined the flashlight on the stream. There was something shiny in the shallow water. He thought it was only a pebble, but his curiosity got the best of him. He went over to it and looked. He saw something, and it sure wasn't a rock.

He shoved his hand into the water. It was so icy cold that he quickly drew his hand back out of the water and thrust his other hand in the frigid depths.

He grabbed hold of the shiny object and pulled it, but it wouldn't move. It was stuck. He would have to move the huge boulder under which it was caught.

He reached over the boulder and tried to pull it toward his body. When it wouldn't budge, he pulled and pulled, trying to rock it back and forth until he finally forced it to move. He reached for the shiny object and yanked it from the frigid water.

He was surprised to see a locket. He opened it and found a picture. He wanted to dry the locket by brushing it against his shirt when he felt how wet his shirt was. He unbuttoned the shirt and let it fall open. The wet shirt was cold against his skin, so he removed it, opting to carry it in his hand when he started for home.

The first thing he had to do was tell Ann. He removed his shoes, entered the house and went directly to Ann's room.

He entered her room, laying his shirt and shoes on the floor. He reached out and put his hand over Ann's mouth. He thought she would scream and, if she did, his family would come running. He didn't want that; he wanted to talk to her alone.

She woke up and froze. She couldn't move because she was too scared. She could feel the cold hand over her mouth. She turned her head to see who it was. When she saw him she let out a sigh, and he removed his hand.

"I didn't mean to scare you, Ann, but I found something I think you ought to see."

"You found something? Where?" she asked, hoping it was a clue.

"In the water where you washed up," he answered.

He reached into his pocket and pulled out the locket. He handed it to her and told her to examine it.

As she opened it she said, "Luke, it's got a picture in it. I think it's a picture of the movie star that got killed. Her picture was in the newspaper. I think her name was Rita something-or-other."

"That isn't much help. A lot of people have a picture of her."

He was sure disappointed. If only it had been a picture of someone else, a family member and not a movie star.

As Luke was preparing to leave Ann's bedside, someone knocked at the door. Luke didn't know what to do. If he were in there when someone came in, they would think bad things of him and Ann. He would be caught in Ann's bedroom without his shirt and shoes at two o'clock in the morning.

He grabbed his shoes and shirt and ran toward the door of the closet, barely closing it before Granny walked into the room.

Ann had her eyes closed, pretending she was asleep.

"I know you're playing possum. You thought you could fool me, didn't you? But you can't. I can always tell when people are playing possum," Granny said as she watched Ann.

Ann opened her eyes.

"I couldn't sleep. I hope I didn't disturb you," Ann said trying to explain away any noises Granny may have heard.

"You didn't disturb me. I couldn't sleep either," said Granny as she tried to hide a yawn.

Granny walked toward the closet but stopped half way. She walked next to the bed and whispered into Ann's ear, "Tell Luke to come out of that closet now."

"You can come out now, Luke," said Ann in a scared whisper.

Luke opened the door and came out carrying his wet shirt and shoes. He looked at Ann, then at Granny.

"Don't look at me that way," said Ann. "I didn't tell."

"Don't worry. I'm not going to tell anyone," said Granny. "All I want to know is where you went, Luke?"

"What are you talking about, Granny?" asked Luke.

"You've got your shoes in your hand. Your shirt is wet, and I know it's not from sweating. You've got the round, scared eyes of someone or something that's been caught in a trap. Now tell me, boy, where did you go?" she whispered harshly as she demanded the truth.

Luke looked to Ann and said, "Ann, we've got to tell Granny."

"Okay," agreed Ann as she glanced away from Luke, trying to hide her fear.

Luke explained about Ann. Granny listened hard because she didn't want to miss a word of it.

After he finished, Granny got up from where she was sitting and walked around the room.

"You mean that you don't know who you are?" she asked.

Ann nodded her head and started to speak when she was interrupted by another knock at the door. Granny and Luke both ran to the closet. It was a tight squeeze, but they both made it inside the closet and out of sight.

Harry knocked again and Ann told him to come in. He entered her room, looked around, and said, "I thought I heard somebody. Are you feeling all right?"

She nodded her head no and said she had a headache.

"I'll get you an aspirin," said Harry.

He left and was back in the room a few moments later. After giving her the aspirin, Harry went to bed.

Granny and Luke came out of the closet.

"That was close," said Luke with a sigh.

Granny started whispering, "Ann, why don't I claim you as a niece? I have relatives all over the country. We could say that your name is Ann Patterson."

"How are you going to explain how I got here? How can you explain why I was so banged and cut up?" asked Ann.

"I'll tell them you got off the Greyhound bus and was walking to our house. You slipped and fell down one of the steep hillsides around here and lost your bearings. That should cover it," said Granny.

Ann didn't know what to say. Why would Granny do that for her? They didn't even know each other.

After Ann glanced again at Granny, who was gazing at her grandson with old eyes filled to the brim with love, she knew what the answer was.

Ann nodded her head yes, and Granny left the room.

Luke stayed in a little while longer and talked.

"If only that locket could talk," said Ann. "I do wish I could remember."

"So do I," said Luke. "So do I."

The next morning, Granny let the family sleep later than usual. Normally they got out of bed at five o'clock, but that day, she didn't wake them until half past six.

"Why did you let us sleep so late? We wasted half the day," mumbled Harry.

"You must have been tired or you would have gotten up on your own," answered Granny. She wasn't about to explain why she had overslept. She didn't want to tell Harry about the conversation she had with Ann about her memory loss. She didn't think he would allow Ann to stay with them if he knew she had lost her memory, especially since Ann wasn't related to them.

Harry was hard to predict at times. Many times she had seen Harry go out of his way to help people. She had seen him give a man his only good shirt so the man had something to wear to his mother's funeral. She had also seen him turn away strangers that were looking for food or a place to sleep for the night without a second thought.

A young girl in trouble and about the same age as his son might cause Harry to have second thoughts about Ann and allowing her to stay in the house, unless she was a family member. Granny, after giving it some thought, decided to give Ann the last name of Patterson, claiming that Ann was the niece she had never met that was always planning to visit.

Harry went to the fields. Emma went to the creek to do the washing, and Granny and Luke stayed home. It was Granny's job to straighten the house and cook. Luke did all the hunting. He provided the family with fresh meat daily for the supper meal, after which he would go help his father with the fieldwork.

After his third cup of coffee, Luke picked up his rifle and left. He would have to shoot something for dinner. He came back around noontime and ate his lunch, then he took Ann for a walk. It couldn't be a long walk because she wasn't strong enough.

Since the movie star, Rita Taylor went over the side of the mountain not far from their house, the people in the area called the spot Lover's Leap because it was rumored that Rita and Bill Taylor had driven off the cliff on purpose in the passion of a fatal fight.

He decided to show it to her. It was the most beautiful place he had ever seen. The side of the mountain was very steep, and at the bottom of the ravine was the river. He could look across the ravine and see the sloping mountainside opposite the one on which he was standing.

Ann wanted to go with him because she wanted to see the place where Rita Taylor had died. She had no idea why that was so important to her, but she really wanted to see that place, to visit it and to find out why it happened.

It took them almost an hour to get to Lover's Leap. Luke walked slowly because Ann was stiff and sore from her accident.

As they arrived at the scene of the accident, out of nowhere came a harsh menacing voice calling, "Annette, Annette, now it's your turn to die."

Ann was startled. She looked at Luke who appeared as startled as she was.

"Who is Annette?" she asked Luke.

"I don't know," he replied in a tension strained voice as he looked around trying to find the point of origin of those frightening words.

"Come closer. I have to drive you off the edge, too. But it won't be in a car," continued the voice.

"Is it talking to me?" asked frightened Ann as she reached for the comfort of Luke.

"I don't know," answered a puzzled Luke. "But we're getting out of here."

He grabbed hold of Ann's hand and started running. They ran all the way home with Luke clutching her hand and pulling her sore body as quickly as he could behind him.

CHAPTER 5

"What's wrong?" asked Granny when she saw their flushed, frightened faces.

She waited a few moments until they could speak.

"Luke, what happened?" she asked again.

"Ann, go lie down and rest. I'll tell Granny what happened."

After Ann left the room, he started his conversation with his grandmother.

"Granny, have you been to the mountain since that movie star went over the edge?"

"Yeah," replied Granny.

"Well, did you hear anything when you were standing there?" he asked.

"Was I supposed to hear something?" she asked. "What was it? What are you talking about, Luke?"

"Did you hear any voices?"

"Nope," she replied. "Don't believe I did. What of it?"

"Well, I took Ann there a little while ago, and we heard something. It was like a ghost," he said. "You couldn't see it, you could only hear it. It was awful scary."

"You must have been imagining things," she laughed. "There ain't no such things as ghosts."

"I know that," said Luke. "But why didn't we see it? All it said was something about a girl named Annette. It said it was going to kill her."

"Hogwash," said Granny. "It was probably someone a trying to play a trick on you. I guess the trick worked, didn't it?"

Granny started doing her housework, and Luke took care of some minor repair jobs around the house. After finishing the repairs Luke went in to check on Ann.

He looked in her room, and she wasn't there.

"Granny, did Ann say where she was going?"

"She didn't say anything to me," replied Granny. "I didn't see her leave."

He went back into Ann's room. The window was open, so she must have crawled through it to the outside.

He went outside and started calling her name. He called and called, but she didn't answer. He didn't know where she could be. Maybe she went back to the mountain?

It was beginning to get dark as he walked toward the mountain. He traveled the same path they had walked earlier.

"Ann! Where are you?" he shouted again and again.

He kept his head up and his mind on guard as he traveled to the cliff where they had heard the voice. As he got closer to the edge of the cliff, he no longer shouted Ann's name.

He peered over the jagged edge of the cliff and stared down into the black depths of the ravine where he could only imagine what it looked like. In his mind, he could see the rocks and boulders that had been worn smooth from hundreds years of weather jutting through the patches of evergreen, consisting mostly of cedar trees that had taken root in the cracks and crevices of the rock. He could hear the sounds of the water as it flowed slowly through the ravine down, far down, the cliff. He could actually see nothing but blackness as it tried to rise up and swallow him whole.

Luke closed his eyes as he listened for Ann to make a sound. He prayed the sound would not rise up and torture his ears from the depths below him.

"Oh-oh-oh!" screamed a voice. "Help me! Help me!"

"Ann, Ann, where are you?" he pleaded.

He was running when he saw her as his heart raced faster at the sight. A man was trying to push her off the side of the mountain a couple of hundred feet from where he was standing.

"Hey you! Leave her alone!" he shouted as he dodged tree branches and jumped over bushes as he tried to reach Ann.

The man heard Luke shout and stopped struggling with Ann.

Luke rushed up to where Ann was standing as she tried to fight off her attacker, but by the time he got there, Ann had fainted and the man was gone.

He picked her up and carried her back to the house.

"Emma, Granny, I need help!" yelled Luke when he arrived at the front door with Ann draped, once again, across his arms.

"What happened?" asked a worried Emma as she rushed ahead of him, clearing the path to the bed on which he needed to place Ann's limp body.

"Someone tried to push her off of the mountain," he explained as he struggled to regain his breath.

"Why?" asked Emma.

"I don't know," he replied with irritation.

"Did you see who was pushing her?" continued Emma.

"It was a man, but I didn't get a very good look at him. It happened too fast. I started running as soon as I saw her struggling, and he disappeared into the trees. I couldn't go after him like I wanted to do. I had to get her back here. God, I hope she's all right."

Luke was near tears as he stared at Ann's lifeless form.

Ann was falling, falling, falling down inside a dark, black cave. She was falling so quickly that she couldn't figure out what was happening to her. The falling sensation filled her mind. It was giving her a light-headed, floating feeling that wasn't fun because it was too fast and too forceful.

"Get out of here," she told herself. "Look for the light."

The falling seemed to slow down until she abruptly stopped. She righted herself in her mind and stood on something. She didn't have any idea what was beneath her feet. It was too dark to be able to make out shapes or forms or see anything at all.

"Look for the light," she told herself.

The darkness smothered her. It covered her like a blanket.

"Look for the light," she said again.

She could see the glow. She floated toward it, gaining speed as she got closer and closer. She was swimming through the smothering darkness, aiming for the glow.

When she woke up, she was as white as the bed sheets on which Luke had placed her unconscious body.

She looked at Luke and started crying.

"I had to go back," she said between sobs. "I just had to go back."

"Why?" asked Luke.

"I don't know," Ann replied.

"Do you know the man that tried to push you off?" he asked.

"He looked familiar but I can't place him," she said.

"Did he say anything to you?"

"Not really. He sort of growled at me telling me to jump. He wanted me to jump off of the side of the mountain, Luke. Why would he want me to do that? Why can't I remember anything? Why is this happening to me?" she asked as she tried to hide her crying face from Luke by rolling over and burying her sobs into the pillow.

He stepped forward and sat beside her on the edge of the bed as he reached his hand out to pull her face away from the pillow, and he scooted himself up toward the headboard against which he

37

leaned. He pulled her head onto his lap and stroked her hair as he tried to soothe her and quiet her tears.

"Ann, it's going to be all right. We'll find the answers. So help me, we'll find out why this is happening," he promised.

He continued to stroke her hair until her breathing became smooth and effortless.

Ann was tired, so he left the room so she could sleep.

He didn't know what to do. Why would anyone want to kill Ann? She was so young and pretty.

* * *

Ann had been staying with the Hamiltons about a month and was enjoying the company of her newly found family. She helped with the chores to pay for her room and board.

"Granny, I've been here for a month, and I still don't have any answers," said Ann sadly.

"Yes, child, but you are welcome to stay as long as you need to," said Granny as she rocked in her special chair and broke the beans she would prepare for supper with a piece of fatback simmered in the same pot to give it some flavor.

"You have all been so good to me," added Ann.

"Well, you do your part around here. You help with the chores and you are good to talk to and look at. Just ask Luke," grinned Granny with a sparkle in her old, tired eyes.

CHAPTER 6

Nina, Annette's best friend, was leaving the orphanage. She was eighteen years of age and finished with high school. She wanted to go to college at night and work in the daytime, but that would have to wait for a while. College wasn't her number one priority. Annette was number one. She had to find her friend.

She was worried. Annette hadn't written her. She was leaving to find out why.

She read the story about Rita Taylor, the movie star, and her husband getting killed. She knew they were Annette's parents. She made a mental note of the name of the lawyer who was mentioned in the article.

As Nina was packing her clothes, Mary Boothe, the supervisor, entered the room.

"I wish you wouldn't go. You know that you'll probably be on a wild goose chase. Annette may not have been in the car."

"I know, but my gut tells me she was, and I have to find out for sure."

Nina thought about that possibility many times. Even if Annette wasn't in the car, where was she? Nina was hoping Annette wasn't in the car because if she was, then Annette's mother and father *and Annette* would be dead, too. That would be terrible.

Annette has been pretty lucky, she thought. *At least she had parents.* Most of the kids in that place didn't even know their parents.

She was two years old when she came to the orphanage. The small life insurance policy she received upon her parents' death was available for her when she turned eighteen. She now had about a thousand dollars, and no one knew about it except the bank and herself.

She withdrew her money from the bank early that morning. She asked the teller for the money in small bills so it wouldn't draw attention along the way. The supervisor always gave the children fifty dollars when they left, so she would also have that to use.

She decided to make a long distance telephone call to find out if Rita's lawyer knew anything about Rita's death or the location of Annette. It took the operator several rings to get an answer, but Nina asked the operator to let it ring until someone picked it up.

"Hello," came a female voice over the telephone.

"Hello," she replied. "My name is Nina Olson. I'm calling about Annette Taylor."

"Who?" the female voice asked.

"Annette Taylor. She is Rita and Bill Taylor's sixteen-year-old daughter," Nina explained.

"Oh, her, what do you want to know?" asked the voice.

"Where is she?" asked Nina.

"I can't tell you that. You'll have to speak to the attorney, and he's not here right now."

Nina explained that Annette was her best friend, that Annette had not written to her and that she was really worried about her.

"I shouldn't tell you but she's at the Sunnnydale Orphanage. She has been staying there practically all of her life. Please don't tell anyone where you got this information. I would get into trouble if you did," explained the female voice.

"I won't tell anyone that you gave me information, but she isn't at the orphanage," said Nina. "She left the orphanage with her parents. They were going to the country in Virginia somewhere. All I want to know is where?"

"You'll have to speak to my boss. If she is not at Sunnydale, I don't know where she is," replied the female voice.

"Thank you," said Nina as she hung up the telephone.

"Virginia," she thought to herself. "I'll just have to go to Virginia."

She asked Mary if she could spend one more day at the orphanage because she needed to make some travel arrangements before she could begin her search for Annette. With Mary's consent she then caught the bus that went to town. She had to keep an eye open for pick pockets or thieves because she didn't want her purse snatched. It had all of her money in it.

She needed to buy a car. It had to be the cheapest one she could find without it falling apart before she drove it off the lot.

At the first car lot she visited, the cheapest car they had was selling for five hundred dollars. It wasn't worth it. The next car lot had a car for three hundred fifty dollars. If she couldn't find a better deal, she was going to buy that one.

She went to the last lot she could find and saw a car there for only two hundred ninety five dollars. The dealer gave her a chance to try it out. It was nice. It was black and had a white convertible top. The man selling the car said he would knock twenty dollars off of the price if she paid cash. The car was no prize-winning beauty. It needed a lot of bodywork, and the convertible top needed to be repaired or replaced, but it hummed when the engine was running.

"I'll have it all cleaned, shined and ready for you to pick up in a few days," said the smiling car dealer.

"That won't do at all. I have to have the car tomorrow because I am going to Virginia to visit a friend. Couldn't you have it ready by tomorrow?" she begged.

"No, miss," he said. "The boys want me to pay them double for overtime, and I can't afford it."

"But I have to have the car tomorrow," she explained.

"I'm sorry, miss," he said walking away. "That's the best I can do."

"Couldn't I pay half of the overtime and you pay half?" she asked hopefully.

"Do you have fifty handy?" he asked.

She reached into her purse and pulled out the money.

"Remember," she said. "I want it early tomorrow morning."

The car dealer smiled and nodded his head.

If she hurried, she could make it just in time to catch the next bus and arrive on time for supper at the orphanage.

Mary told the other children about Nina going away, and they all decided they wanted to give Nina a party.

When Nina walked in to eat dinner, no one was there. The table was cleared, and there wasn't a sound. At first, the quietness scared her. She didn't know what to think.

All at once from out of nowhere came a sneeze, and then lots of "shushes" followed.

"Where are you?" she asked as she glanced around under tables and other obvious hiding spots. "I know you're around here somewhere."

"Surprise!" they all yelled in unison.

"We wanted to give you a going away party and a birthday party," piped one voice.

A surprise going away and birthday party. That thought had not entered her mind. It was a big and wonderful surprise.

Swarms of children formed a circle to sing "Happy Birthday." She was so happy all she could do was cry. The children even bought her a few gifts. To them it was like losing a big sister.

One of her gifts was a beautiful sweater. The five children who pooled their money to buy it handed it to her and each gave her a big kiss. There were several small gifts; even a gift from the janitor. There were handkerchiefs and bottles of perfume everywhere.

"Where are you going?" asked Billy.

"I'm going to Virginia," she answered.

"What for?" asked Billy

"To look for someone."

"Who?" probed Billy.

"My best friend, Annette," she answered slowly. "You all know Annette. She went to Virginia with some people, and she hasn't come back. She promised to write to me and it has been over a month since she left."

"Do you think someone kidnapped her?" asked many little voices with concerned faces.

"No. They didn't kidnap her but I'm going to find her anyway. Stop asking me all these questions. Let's have some fun."

"Look! They're serving ice cream and cake," someone yelled. "And you're to be the first one served."

"Listen kids. Why don't we give thanks to the Lord for all the wonderful things he has done?" she said pausing until the other kids were served.

"What we got to be thankful for?" asked a small voice. "We ain't got no mama and papa. So what we got to be thankful for?"

"Listen, Jeremiah," she said softly. "There was only one person here whose real parents wanted her. Do you remember Annette? Of course you do. Everybody remembers her. She was the one with her real parents. She's the one I'm going to look for. You know the movie star that died? Her name was Rita Taylor, and she was killed in an automobile accident along with her husband. They were Annette's parents. Something terrible could have happened to Annette because she was with them. They were going to Virginia for a vacation. In the paper there was no mention of a girl being dead, too. So you can be thankful you're alive because she might not be."

"Why ain't anybody looking for her?" asked Jeremiah.

"Because," continued Nina. "There were just a few people who knew who she was. Our Miss Mary, the Taylors' lawyer and I were the only ones who knew."

"I hope you find her," said Jeremiah very much ashamed of himself.

"All you kids bow your heads," she said as she bowed hers.

"Dear Lord. We are thankful for all the things you have done for us. Help and watch over us. Please Lord, help Annette wherever she may be. I ask these things in thy holy name. Amen."

"All right kids, you had better eat your ice cream before it melts," she said.

After they finished, Nina told the children to wash up and go to bed.

Jeremiah walked toward Nina and said, "Nina, will you say a prayer with me tonight before going to bed?"

"Of course, I will," she replied.

She was surprised. Never before had she been asked to say a prayer with anyone. They all considered what they said to be a secret to be shared only with God.

When bedtime arrived, Nina stood at Jeremiah's bedside.

"What are you going to say in your prayer?" she asked as she kneeled next to Jeremiah and watched as the seven-year-old searched for words to say.

"What should I say?" he asked.

"Do you have something that's really, really important for you to get an answer to? Suppose that maybe your parents are still alive, and maybe yours are, would you want to ask God to lead them to you?"

"No, I don't think so. If they wanted me, I wouldn't be here."

"Maybe you're right about that. Okay, do you have a sick friend who needs help? You could ask God to lend a hand and help make your friend all better."

44

"No, I know what I'll say. Dear God, please help Nina find her friend. Amen."

"That's a great prayer, Jeremiah. Thanks for asking God to help me," Nina said as she hugged Jeremiah and tucked him under the covers. She brushed his forehead with a gentle kiss before saying goodnight.

After saying the prayer with Jeremiah, she collected her birthday presents and went to bed. She would pack them in a box when she got out of bed the next morning so she could take all of the wonderful gifts with her.

She was about to fall asleep when the telephone rang. When she answered it, someone asked for Lucille Dooley. She knocked on Lucille's door telling her that she had a telephone call.

Nina thought it was stupid calling someone after midnight. She went back to bed and was having a beautiful dream when the telephone rang again. She went to the telephone practically in her sleep. The person asked for Lucille, and before she heard last name, Nina was knocking on Lucille's door.

One more time Nina went back to bed, but the telephone rang a third time. She wanted to let it ring, but if she did it would wake up everybody.

"Hello," she said with a great deal of irritation mixed into her voice.

"Hello," said a muffled male voice. "May I speak to Nina Olson? It's very urgent."

"Wait a minute. I'll get...Who?"

"Nina Olson," said the impatient voice.

"Oh, oh, that's me. I thought you wanted to speak to a girl that has been getting phone calls left and right," she said now wide awake.

"Miss Olson," said the mysterious voice. "I have a message for you."

"What kind of message?" she asked anxiously fearing the worst.

"It's regarding Annette Taylor."

"Where is she? Who are you? Do you know her?" asked Nina.

"Calm yourself," said the voice. "And just listen. Annette is safe. She is very happy where she is. She is living on a farm in southern Virginia. But, she will be killed if anyone finds her. Do you hear me? I said she will be killed."

Suddenly the telephone was dead. Nina was too frightened to do anything. She stood there with the receiver in her hand. She finally hung it up, and as she did it rang again.

She stood there and let it ring. It kept ringing until Mary came out of her room to answer it. Nina turned around, saw her coming, and fainted.

Mary picked up the telephone and heard someone laughing. Then the line was dead. She hung it up with a disgusted look on her face. A thought came to her that it was some practical joker that had frightened the poor girl to death.

She knocked on the doors of some of the rooms and asked for help in getting Nina back to her room. She was worried about Nina. It didn't take very long for Nina to wake up from her faint. When she opened her eyes, she screamed.

"They can't kill her!"

Nina looked around and realized her room was filled with people standing around her.

"Kill who, dear?" asked the worried Mary.

"Oh, no one," said Nina. "I must have been having a nightmare."

Mary knew differently. She chased the rest of the kids back to their rooms and came back to have a nice long talk with Nina.

When they were alone, Nina burst into tears.

"Nina, I know something was said on the telephone to upset you. I want to know what it was," said Mary as she tried to console Nina.

"Well, I might as well tell you. The phone rang, and I went to answer it. I thought it was for Lucille. She had already received two calls. Then the voice asked for me. At first I didn't realize it because I was half-asleep. The voice said it had a message for me. It said that Annette would be killed if I looked for her. It said she was living in southern Virginia on a farm. That was all it said."

"It must have been a joke," said Mary. "After you fainted I answered the telephone, and I heard someone laughing. It could have been a mean practical joke."

"I don't think it was," said Nina thoughtfully. "After all, there are just a few people that knew about Annette."

"Well, I think you should get some rest now," Mary said.

After Mary left the room Nina couldn't sleep. She kept thinking about Annette. Annette's birthday was coming up in a few days, and she would be seventeen. Annette had already graduated from high school because she was double promoted in one of the grades. It was very unusual for a person to graduate when they were sixteen.

Finally at the crack of dawn, Nina went to sleep.

Mary slipped in to see about her. Nina had set the alarm to ring at seven o'clock, but Mary changed the setting to eight to allow her some extra sleep. Leaving an hour later wouldn't hurt her.

At eight o'clock the alarm rang. Nina looked at it and was surprised. She thought she had set it for seven.

Oh well, an hour won't make any difference, she thought as she jumped from bed and started packing her things. She was making the bed when she was startled by the telephone ringing. She went to answer it.

"Hello," she said cheerfully.

"Miss Olson," said the voice. "Remember what I said."

"Who are you? Why do you want to hurt Annette?"

The telephone was suddenly dead. She realized what had happened during the night wasn't a dream. It was real!

When she went downstairs to eat her breakfast, the kids crowded around her and asked her questions about fainting. She told them she fainted just for the fun of it.

She told them she took twenty deep breaths, stuck her thumb in her mouth, and blew on it as hard as she could. She had to tell them something other than what really happened. She knew what she said would never make them faint. All it would do is make them a little lightheaded.

She finished breakfast and was starting back to her room when Mary stopped her.

"Nina. I don't think it's safe for you to go searching for Annette. We'll call the police, and let them do it."

"They won't do anything," said Nina.

"Why not? We'll report her as a missing person. That should get them interested," replied Mary.

"Missing from where, Mary?" asked Nina, exasperated.

"What do you mean?"

"She was with her parents, and they didn't acknowledge her existence. They're dead, so how can they report her missing?"

"She lives here in this facility," said Mary.

"Yes, but you let the orphan girl leave with two famous people who claimed to be her parents. How do you think that will look for you?" said Nina.

"You've got a point. I'm not supposed to tell anybody about Annette's family. But they're dead, what would it matter?"

"The telephone call makes it matter. What if whoever called me finds out that we called the police? Would he kill Annette before anyone had a chance to find her?"

"This is dangerous, Nina!" exclaimed Mary.

"I know, but what choice do I have? Annette's my best friend and I've got to help her. What if she hadn't told me about her parents? Nobody would be looking for her," said an anxious Nina.

"When did she tell you about her parents?" asked Mary.

"I caught sight of her putting her suitcase in the car, and she chose not to lie to me because we're best friends. Now, I'm choosing to find her, my best friend," said a tearful Nina.

"I wish everybody in this whole wide world could have a best friend like you, Nina. This world would be a much better place to live if we all looked after each other," replied Mary.

"You would do the same for your best friend, wouldn't you?" asked Nina, smiling through the tears.

"I would like to think that I would," replied Mary.

"Well, I've got to go finish packing," said Nina as she stuffed her suitcase.

"Please write or call me, Nina. Let me know what's happening. Okay?"

Nina shook her head in response to Mary's request and hugged her supervisor tightly. Nina wanted Mary to know she would miss her.

Nina decided she would finish packing and go pick up her car. They should have finished the requested repairs. She hoped she had paid them enough for the rush job.

It was about ten o'clock before she could get away from the orphanage and onto the bus headed to the dealer to pick up her car and begin her search.

When she got into the car, it didn't look like the same one. The salesman said Mary found out about it and had them practically rebuild it when he had called to verify a repair to be made that would cost a bit more than anticipated.

It had been painted, the canvas top was replaced plus new tires and seat covers were added. They put in new spark plugs, and all the other things they could replace under the hood except a new motor. He handed her the keys.

She got in, and there on the seat was a large envelope. In it was a hundred dollars and a note. The children gave it to her out of the money they had earned.

49

She would be all alone. There wouldn't be anybody with her to tell her what to do. She had to think on her own. She had to act on her own. The idea of being alone frightened her. At the orphanage there were always people around. She was also frightened for Annette.

What would they do to Annette if she found her? Why wouldn't Annette write? Was she really happy like the voice said, or was she being held captive by someone? Nina hoped and prayed she wasn't. But if she wasn't, where could she be? She didn't have any family except for her mother and father, and they were both dead. What a terrible thing to happen to such a sweet girl.

Nina drove along until she found herself getting tired, so she stopped for coffee and to stretch her legs.

"Coffee, please," she said to the tired-eyed woman behind the counter.

"Anything else?" asked the worker.

"No, just coffee," said Nina.

Nina looked around the little diner with a curious eye.

The place looked old and worn, but it was clean and sparkly in all the right places.

Next to Nina, who was sitting in front of the counter, was a man engrossed in a conversation with another man positioned next to him. Nina could hear only bits and pieces of their conversation.

"...Rita Taylor, the movie star. She was pregnant...read in the newspaper."

Immediately Nina was at full attention, straining as much as she could to eavesdrop.

"Yeah, I heard about that. It happened not too far from here.

"...seen it?"

"No."

"...it sure was a steep...cops said brakes gave out..."

"It must have been an accident then," said the man sitting next to Nina. She could hear almost everything he was saying. She wasn't able to hear the other man very clearly.

"Well...heard it was on purpose... fight...drove off cliff..."

She wanted to jump into the exchange of words, but she was afraid that one of those men or both of them were the ones who had threatened her. She wanted to question both men and find out if they really knew anything about the accident or were merely repeating gossip. Fearful, she decided against approaching either of the strangers.

After drinking the coffee, she went back to the car. She drove until it got dark and then looked for a cheap motel. She wanted to save her money, so she got the cheapest room they had to offer.

It was a mess. It was like walking into a pigsty. It had a rotten smell to it. She opened the window to let the fresh air in. It helped a little but not enough.

It was getting late, and she was so tired that she went straight to bed. She didn't stay in the bed for very long because of the bed bugs. She got up and went to the sofa. She thought she could get some rest on that, but she was mistaken. The springs kept jabbing her in the back.

She decided her car would make a better bed. She collected her things and went back to the car. After putting the luggage away, she went to the manager's office.

"May I speak to the manager?" she inquired at the desk.

"What for?" asked the man she had spoken to earlier.

"What for?" she said sarcastically. "What do you mean what for? I want my money back. No one can stay in that awful room."

"All right, lady," said the desk clerk. "I'll get him."

He slipped through the door directly behind the desk. She waited and waited. She thought he would never return.

"Lady," he said. "Step right in here." He motioned to the door behind him.

She went through the doorway and was flabbergasted at what she saw. The room was exquisitely decorated. It was really beautiful. She stood in the doorway with her mouth open as she looked around her absorbing the beauty.

"You had better shut your mouth, or you might catch a fly," chuckled an elderly man behind a large desk.

"What? Oh, I'm sorry, Mr.?" she said as she blushed.

"John. My name is John. What was this I heard about you not being satisfied?" he asked.

"Well, I was going to ask for my money back. The room I got was a complete mess. There were bed bugs, and the sofa was very uncomfortable. My name is Nina, by the way," she said angrily.

"How much did you pay?" asked the elderly man.

"Ten dollars," she replied. "I'm not the richest girl in the world."

"You got the worst room in the motel. The guests who stay in that room bring the bugs with them. I'll have to exterminate again," he said apologetically. "We only give it to people who look like they can't afford the twenty-five dollar room."

"Is the twenty-five dollar room better?" asked Nina.

"Yes, of course. It's a lot better," he replied. "The twenty-five dollar rooms have carpets and everything you need such as a telephone, a television and a radio. No stereo though, but I'm getting one for all the good rooms pretty soon."

"Do you have anymore twenty-five dollar rooms available?" asked Nina.

"Yes, I think we have one left. Would you like it?" asked the man.

"I don't know if I'll like it or not," she replied hotly.

John picked up a key and escorted her out of the office. He walked to the elevator and pushed the button. She followed, and the elevator stopped at the third floor. It was cool on the third floor, not hot and sticky like it had been in the room she had rented for ten dollars.

John walked to the end of the cool hall and unlocked the door. She went inside and was very pleased with what she saw. She reached into her purse for the balance of the money, but the elderly man brushed at her hand.

"Oh, don't bother about the money," he said. "It's on the house."

"I'll pay for the room," explained Nina.

"No, I don't want or need your money. But you're welcome to stay," he said.

"Thank you," she said sweetly. "I will stay and hopefully get a good night's sleep."

She walked with him to the elevator. She turned and walked to the door beneath the exit sign before she realized she could have taken the elevator down to the first floor, too. *Oh well, the exercise won't hurt*, she thought as she ran down the steps.

She walked out to her car and pulled out her suitcase. Before she left the parking lot, she locked her car to be sure it would be parked in the same spot the next morning.

Nina went back into the motel, and this time she rode the elevator. She unpacked what she would wear the next morning. After deciding on a blue skirt and white blouse, she went to the bathroom, brushed her teeth and climbed into bed. She fell asleep immediately, because she was thoroughly exhausted.

CHAPTER 7

While Ann stayed with the Hamiltons, she began to take on more chores around the farm. She and Luke always helped each other with their work so they could have more time together. If Luke was finished with his chores and Ann wasn't, he would help her as best he could. They went for long walks, and sometimes they went fishing. Every once in a while, Luke would take her hunting with him.

Since Harry did most of the fieldwork, and Luke did the hunting, Luke usually had time on his hands.

One Monday morning, Luke and Ann were both restless. He finished what he was doing and came in to help Ann. He washed the dishes while she dried them and put them away. When they were finished, he grabbed up his rifle, and they were on their way. They wanted to go for a walk. Luke always took his gun in case they ran across some good game.

As they were walking along, Ann tripped and fell. Luke tried to help her up, but she said she couldn't put any pressure on her ankle. He picked her up gently and walked until she told him to put her down. When he did, she stood on her foot as if nothing had happened. He looked at her and then his face turned red.

"You little sneak," he said. "Of all the tricks. You're just lazy."

"I just wanted to see if you would carry me. You did, too," she said as she smiled.

"This isn't the first time I've had to carry you. I had to carry you twice before in case you don't remember," he reminded her.

He stepped toward her and put his strong arms around her small waist. She turned her face to his. He kissed her tenderly. Ann pulled away and started walking back home. She limped a little.

She and Luke discussed things they knew about her, which was very little. He asked her if she remembered anything yet. She shook her head sadly. She couldn't remember a thing. She was several yards away from the house when she stopped to ask him a question.

"Luke, will you do me a favor?" she asked.

"Yeah," he replied. "What is it?"

"Hit me," she said with a serious face.

"Hit you? I wouldn't hit you!" he exclaimed.

"Why not?" she asked.

"Because I think too much of you to want to hurt you," he replied softly.

"Please hit me," she begged. "I read somewhere that people with amnesia can get hit on the head a second time, and it might bring back their memory."

"Don't be silly," he laughed. "I'm not going to hit you, and I never will."

They got back to the house barely in time for supper. After dinner, Emma and Ann washed the dishes while Luke, Granny and Harry sat down to talk.

"When is Ann going back?" asked Harry. The question took Granny by surprise.

"I'll let Ann answer that," replied Granny.

Then she went into the kitchen and spoke with Ann. She returned to the room with Ann in tears.

"What's wrong?" asked Harry.

"In the first place," said Granny. "Ann is not my relative; at least, not that I know of. In the second place, she doesn't know who she is."

"What? Why didn't you tell me?" he shouted angrily.

He was stunned. Why hadn't they told him? Why did they keep it a secret from him?

"We didn't tell you because we knew you would object to her staying here," explained Granny. "And we didn't want that to happen."

"Can she stay with us until we find out who she is? Someone's got to help her," pleaded Emma.

"It's okay with me. We can help her all we can," said a resigned Harry.

Ann was happy. Now she didn't have anything to hide. They all knew about her not remembering. She didn't feel very well, so she picked up an old magazine to read before she went to bed. She was looking through the magazine when an article caught her eye. It was about Rita Taylor. It said something about a daughter in an orphanage. Then it showed a couple of pictures of where the accident happened. It also said that if they couldn't find the daughter, the lawyer would inherit all the money.

Ann wondered why the name Rita Taylor was so familiar. She had seen the place where Rita and her husband were killed. As a matter of fact, someone tried to kill her at the same spot. Maybe the person thought she was someone else. Maybe that person knew who she really was.

She decided she needed to go back to the mountain the next day to look around. After reading the article, she turned out the light and went to sleep. She started tossing and turning and screaming in her sleep. Luke heard her and came running to see what was wrong. He woke her up and held her until she stopped trembling.

"What were you dreaming about, Ann?" Luke asked in a whisper when the trembling stopped.

"I don't want to talk about it now. You don't mind, do you? It was so scary that I don't even want to think about it. Can I tell you in the morning?" she pleaded weakly.

"Sure, honey, no problem," he answered as he kissed her softly on her wrinkled brow. The tension and fear still registered on her face. Luke kissed her lips tenderly and got up to leave. He closed the door as he left the room and found Granny pretending to doze on a chair in the hall. She smiled and went back to her room. Luke didn't know what she was smiling about, so he followed her. He went into Granny's room, turned on the light and sat on the edge of the bed.

"What were you smiling about?" he asked Granny.

"You," she said. "You looked real funny when you came out of her room. Like you was on cloud nine or something."

"What do you mean, Granny? I looked like I always look," he sputtered.

"You sure did," she laughed. "You looked like you always do when you're around her."

"What's that supposed to mean?" he asked as his face turned red.

"Well, it's just you don't act like yourself when she's around you. So get on out of here so I can go back to bed," she said pushing him out the door.

Luke had a restless night of sleep because he worried about Ann and her nightmare. Why was it too scary to talk about when she woke up screaming?

As soon as he was dressed the next morning, he went in search of Ann and an explanation. He located her in the kitchen alone, fortunately, so he could ask her a few questions without the thoughts and ideas of others being interjected.

"What happened last night?" he asked.

"Good morning, Luke," replied Ann.

"I'm sorry," said Luke. "Good morning, Ann. Now about last night?"

"What about it?" she asked.

"What caused you to scream?" he wanted to know.

"I had a nightmare," she explained.

"I figured that out, but what was it about?" he asked again.

"It was about falling into a cave and not being able to find my way out," she said.

"Do you think it might be important to your memory problem?" he asked.

"I don't think so. I don't know really," she said.

"What happened in your dream?" he asked.

"I told you," she said. "It was about falling in a black cave. It was so dark and so black that I lost my perspective. I couldn't find my footing so I couldn't find my way out."

"What made you scream?" he asked.

"Panic, I guess. I had no solid ground to stand on and no light to aim for, so I had no way out of the darkness. It scared me, Luke."

"I'm sure it did," he replied thoughtfully. "But you're safe now."

"I know, but I don't know who I am," she said.

"You'll get your memory back someday," he assured her.

"Yeah, someday," she said.

"Don't get discouraged," he added.

"I can't help it, Luke. Now, get out of here so I can start breakfast."

At the breakfast table, Harry made an announcement, "I'm taking Ann to town to see a doctor. I want the doctor to tell me what can be done to help her."

"I will go with you," said Luke in rapid response to his father's statement.

It wasn't very often that Luke went to town because they lived so far away that it took valuable time away from survival chores when they traveled that long road.

Harry went outside to hitch up the old haywagon that they used around the farm. Ann liked the horse-drawn wagon better than the car, so he always took it when she went anywhere with them, and when the weather was good, he let her drive it. It was a fun thing to do when the weather permitted the pleasure. It was a two hour ride in the haywagon, but it was wonderful.

When they arrived at the doctor's office, they had to wait a little while before Dr. Trent, the new doctor in town, could see them. Finally the doctor made an appearance.

"I didn't have any appointments scheduled today. Who are you and why are you here?" asked the doctor as his eyes scanned the three people standing in front of him.

"We needed to talk to you about this young lady," said Harry as he pointed to Ann.

"She looks like a healthy female specimen to me. Is this an emergency?" asked Dr. Trent as his eyes searched Ann's outward appearance from head to toe.

"We wouldn't be here if we didn't think it was necessary," answered an irritated Harry.

"Let me give you the name, address and telephone number for the doctor who is going to be caring for my patients while I'm on vacation," he said as he writes the information on a scrap piece of paper.

"This doctor is twenty miles further on up the road. We brought the wagon. We can't go see him," said Harry angrily.

"My family's waiting for me in the car. Next time make an appointment," said Dr. Trent as he steered Harry, Luke and Ann toward the door.

"How do you think we can do that, Dr. Trent?" asked Luke. "We don't have a telephone, and how can we predict that we're going to be sick?"

"I'm sorry, but I've got to go," said the impatient doctor.

Luke was angry when he left the doctor's office. He stomped out through the reception room and slammed the door as hard as he could.

Ann was angry, too, but she didn't express it like Luke did. She calmly walked out. As she was going, though, she gave the nurse a mean look.

They climbed up onto the haywagon and headed for home. Ann was driving, Harry was in the middle and Luke was swearing under his breath on the other side of Harry.

Ann saw the lake along the route and got an idea. She leaned over and whispered the idea to Harry. Harry nodded in agreement, so she started driving off the road. Luke was on the side next to the lake. Ann drove the horse-drawn wagon as close as she could get to the water and then changed places with Harry. Harry could hardly keep from laughing.

Luke was so busy thinking and muttering and mumbling that he didn't notice Harry and Ann had changed places. She, with the help of Harry, shoved Luke as hard as she could. Luke landed in the shallow water.

"What did you do that for?" he asked as he looked up at Ann with shock plastered on his face.

Harry and Ann were laughing so hard they didn't notice him getting out of the water. Ann stopped laughing long enough to see Luke reach up and grab her around the waist. He pulled her off the wagon and carried her to the edge of the water. She kicked and screamed.

"Put me down, Luke, please!"

"No, little lady, you're going to get a dunk in the water," he said.

He waded into the water until it came to his knees and stopped. Ann wasn't kicking and screaming anymore.

"Luke, please take me back to the wagon," she pleaded.

"I don't think so. Not yet anyway. Can you take what you dish out?" he asked as he lifted her as high as his shoulders, and then with all his strength he threw her as hard as he could.

She fell into the water that was over her head, and with all of the clothes she had on, it was pretty hard to swim. Luke noticed she was having trouble, so he went out after her. He carried her back to the bank, and they both laughed and laughed.

Harry was getting tired of waiting for them and said he was going to leave without them. They climbed onto the wagon, and Harry told the horse to move. When they arrived home their clothes were almost dry.

"What happened to you two?" asked Granny as she stared at Luke and Ann.

"We went for a swim in the lake," answered Luke with a grin.

"With all your clothes on?" she asked, confused.

"Yeah, we did," he said with a grin on his face.

"It's all my fault, Granny," said Ann as she laughed at the reflection of the two of them the mirror hanging on the wall.

"She started it by shoving me off the wagon into the lake. I finished it by pulling her from the wagon and throwing her into the water with me," explained Luke.

"You're a mess," grumbled Granny as she fussed around the room. She was grumbling because she didn't get to see all the fun, not because it was something that shouldn't have happened.

"They're washable, Granny," said Harry in a calming tone. "No harm's been done."

Ann went to her room to change clothes. When she came back, she helped unhitch the wagon. It wasn't hard to do, but when she was finished she was exhausted.

She helped with supper, and after eating and doing the dishes, she went to bed. When she tried to go to sleep, she couldn't. All she could do was worry. She thought that if they couldn't help her find out who she was, then she would have to do it herself.

She would go to the mountain the next day. She would ask Luke to go with her. If he wouldn't go, then she was going would go alone.

CHAPTER 8

She got up early the next morning and saddled a horse. When she came back into the house Luke was up and sitting at the kitchen table.

"I'm going for a ride, Luke. You want to come?"

"Where to?" he asked.

"To the mountain," she said. "I want to look around some more."

"Someone tried to push you off that mountain. Why do you want to go back there?"

"I want to know why," she said.

"It won't take long, will it? I've got to do my chores, and so do you."

"No, not long," she said. "I'll go alone if I have to."

"No, no, don't do that. I'll come with you," he said as they walked out to the barn together. He got his horse, and she waited until it was saddled and ready to go.

It took them thirty minutes to reach the mountaintop. Ann immediately dismounted and started going down the steep side of the mountain. She had seen something glinting in the sunlight and wanted to know what it was.

"Ann, come back. That spot is too steep to be climbing down without a rope or something," he yelled as she continued to make her way down the steep ravine. He was half-way to her when she stopped and reached down to where she had seen the object.

She picked it up and looked to see if Luke had seen her. The object was a small change purse. Inside of it was fifty dollars and a piece of paper with three phone numbers written on it. Luke was coming so she crammed it into her pocket and acted as though she was looking for something else. She picked up a piece of glass and looked at it.

"Did you find something?" asked Luke as he struggled to return to normal breathing.

"Just a piece of glass. See?" she said as she threw it back to the ground.

"Did it have any writing on it?" he asked.

"It looked like it belonged to an old soda bottle and had been lying on the ground for a long time," she said, acting uninterested.

"I was hoping you had found something," he said in a disappointed tone.

"So was I. Let's get back up the hillside," she said.

She started climbing back up the cliff. Going up was a lot harder than coming down. She slipped a couple of times and almost fell all the way back down. She would have if Luke hadn't stopped her from sliding so she could gain control of her balance.

They rode home without saying a word. All Ann could think about was the change purse. Who did it belong to? What was it doing down there? She decided that she would wait until the following morning to go to the public telephone about a mile up the road and make three telephone calls.

When they got back to the house, Luke went hunting, and Ann didn't have anything to do, so she decided to follow him for the fun of it. He taught her how to shoot a rifle, so she grabbed the one that belonged to Harry that was propped against the wall in the corner behind the front door. She met up with Luke. He was already on his way home with a rabbit he had shot for dinner.

"Hey, Luke," shouted a smiling Ann.

"What are you doing here?" he asked, surprised.

"I just wanted to see if I could find you," she said.

"Is there anything wrong?"

"No, I just wanted to talk. That's all," she said.

"Okay. What do you want to talk about?" he asked.

"About me, about you and about us," she said.

"What about you, me and us?" he asked.

"I need to find out who I am. You need to know who I am. There can't be an us without those answers," she explained.

"I know, I know," he agreed as he placed his strong arms around her holding her next to him. She could feel the love traveling though his body reaching out for her.

"I don't care who or what you are, Ann. You know that don't you?"

"I do, Luke. I need to know."

Luke brushed his lips gently against her forehead as he released her from his hug. She had been planning to tell Luke about the change purse she had found but decided against that decision for the moment.

"One little rabbit isn't enough for supper unless we make a stew. Let's get another one so we can fry them and eat a good supper."

Luke shot two more rabbits, and she shot a squirrel before they started home. After cleaning the fresh game, Ann went in to help get dinner.

She didn't eat much. All she could think about was the change purse. There were three telephone numbers, and they all looked like long distance. She had only a dollar in change. Would that be enough money for all three calls? The three telephone numbers were Glendale 5-9001, Florida 8-9562, and Ontario 1-9110.

Of course, she had fifty dollars, but she couldn't spend it. After all, she didn't know to whom the money belonged.

CHAPTER 9

Nina had been driving a lot, stopping to ask questions in every small town she passed through, and her money was dwindling fast. She began to think she would never find Annette. She would keep looking until she ran out of money.

She hadn't been eating very much and was losing weight rapidly. She couldn't afford to eat more than one meal a day. Sometimes she skipped the one meal to save money.

She stopped at a motel. She usually got a good room but didn't have to pay a lot. They would take one look at her and know she didn't have much money. They could see how pale and sick she was. Sometimes they would even give her a free meal.

She didn't like the idea of not paying for her food, but she just couldn't afford it. The clerk asked her to wait, then he went through the door behind the counter. She waited and waited. He finally came back with another man.

"I'm Roger Mason," said the man.

"I'm Nina Olson. I was asking your clerk for a cheap room, so I could get a shower and go to sleep on a bed, not in my car."

Roger nodded his head, and the clerk saw him. He reached for the keys on the wall behind him. The key he was getting was on the top. Roger picked up her bag and was going to take her to her room.

"I can carry that," she said. "If you point the way, I can find the room. You don't need to bother."

He kept on walking as though he hadn't heard her. He went to the elevator and pushed the button for the fifth floor. Nina thought it would never stop. She kept going up and up. When it did stop, it jolted slightly and knocked her down.

"I'm going to have to get this elevator checked," said Roger as he reached to help her up. She put her hand in his, and he placed his arm around her waist. He lifted her gently. Outside the elevator door, he picked up her bags and took her to her room.

"It's this way, Nina," he said gently.

She nodded in agreement and followed him without uttering a word. She was astonished when she saw her room. It was beautiful. It was the prettiest room she had ever seen. There were big plush green carpets, a telephone, a radio and a television. She turned to Roger.

"How much is this? I can't afford it," she said as she started to leave.

He stopped her by touching her arm.

"I knew you couldn't afford it, but you looked as if you needed rest and food," he said.

"But, but, I can't take this," she sputtered. "How could I pay you?"

"Well, to me you look like you've got an honest face. You could send it to me, or you could get a job in town," he said.

She didn't know what to do. She did like the room, and she knew she would eventually have to get a job and start a new life outside of the orphanage.

"That's all. I don't have to do anything else?" she asked.

"That's it," he replied.

"All right," she said. "I'll stay here tonight, but I'm going to get a job and pay you for it."

Roger went back into the elevator. She closed the door and took off her shoes. She wanted to walk on the plush carpet with her bare feet. She had almost asked him how much it cost to stay in the room for the night. She didn't ask because she was afraid he would tell her an outrageous price that she would never be able to pay. She wanted to enjoy the room in blissful ignorance.

She went in the luxurious bedroom where beautiful lamps were on the dresser with a large mirror. The bed felt soft and comfortable with nice clean white sheets. She sat on the bed a minute and went exploring again.

The kitchen area was small but nice. She was so tired that all she could think of was the comfortable bed. After she showered and changed into her pajamas, she crawled into bed where, as soon as her head touched the pillow, she was asleep.

She woke up when she heard someone knocking on her door. She went to see who it was. She opened the door and looked. She didn't see anyone, so she went out into the hall to look. Still there was no one. She started to go inside when she saw the envelope. She stooped to pick it up. It had the name Nina Olson typed on it.

She didn't know why she would get a letter because no one knew she was here. She yanked the envelope open and saw that it wasn't typed inside but that the note had been written by words cut from newspapers and magazines.

Dear Miss Olson

I told you to quit looking for Annette Taylor

Now I'm going to kill her because you have not done

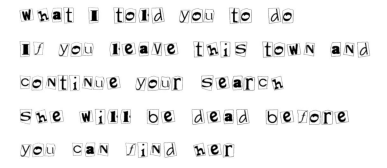

What I told you to do
If you leave this town and
continue your search
She will be dead before
you can find her

The Messenger

Nina was so scared she couldn't move. Would he actually kill Annette? Was it a he? She decided she would go to the police. What if he followed her? Would he kill Annette?

Then she thought of having the police come to her room. If he knew where she was, he would know they came. What was she going to do?

She got dressed and made some coffee. She couldn't eat. Her stomach was grinding from all the acids stirred by worry. She paced back and forth, back and forth. She didn't know what to do.

She called Roger and asked him to come up to her room if he wasn't too busy. She had to talk to someone.

After a few minutes Roger was whistling merrily as he knocked on Nina's door. He had been waiting for her to call him. If she hadn't called him then, he would have called her and invited her to breakfast.

"Come in, Roger," she said. "Please have a seat."

He didn't know what to say because she had such a glum look on her face.

"Roger," she said. "If I tell you something, would you keep it a secret?"

Roger blushed. She would probably tell him she was married and that her husband was going to kill her. That's the line all the beautiful girls used when they didn't want to be bothered. But she didn't look like the type to run away. She looked as if when she got married it would be for always.

"Yes," he answered solemnly.

She got up, went to her purse and got the note. She paused as though she wasn't sure she could trust him. After a second's thought, she decided she could. She had to trust someone. She had no one else, so she handed him the note.

"I need some help," she said. "Could you help me?"

He was taken by surprise. He read the note and immediately got up to leave.

"Don't go," she pleaded.

"Why?" he asked, angrily.

"Because I need your help," she said, eyes wide.

"It doesn't look like you need help to me. You probably made up this note, so I would help you hide from your husband," he said angrily.

"My husband?" she screamed. "I don't even have a husband! I'm not married!"

He looked at her. She was going to burst into tears any second now. She looked as though she was really scared.

"What's this all about?" he asked skeptically as sat down again.

The tears started. She couldn't help it. She had to cry. Roger tried to console her, but it was no use.

"Things can't be that bad. Tell me everything, Nina," he said as he reached for her hands to hold them in his protective grip. She cried and cried. When she couldn't cry any more, she told him what happened.

"I have a friend," she began. "My best friend, whose name is Annette Taylor. We've lived in an orphanage like sisters for as long as I can remember. Annette told me that she was going on vacation in Virginia with her mom and dad."

"Wait a minute. I thought you said you lived in an orphanage?" Roger interrupted.

"I did say that. I am an orphan, but I found out the day Annette left for her trip that she wasn't an orphan. She explained that she was living at Sunnydale to stay out of the public eye and away from the hounding reporters and fan magazines. You see, her mother is Rita Taylor, the actress."

"Rita Taylor died recently. A car accident wasn't it?" he asked.

"Yes, that's why I'm looking for Annette. They didn't say anything about her daughter or that a third person was involved in the car wreck."

"She probably wasn't with them," he speculated.

"I know she was, because I saw her get into the car with them. Only her mother and father were killed. Only two bodies were found," she explained.

"So now you're trying to find her," he reasoned.

"Yes," she answered as she struggled to hold back the tears that filled her eyes.

"Where did the note come from?" he asked.

"That's my problem," she replied. "I don't know."

"Who knew you were looking for Annette Taylor?" asked Roger.

"Mary Boothe, the supervisor at Sunnydale Orphanage. And of course, anyone that I questioned along the way would know," Nina answered.

"Is that the only threat you received?" Roger continued to question her.

"No, I received a couple of telephone calls at Sunnydale saying almost the same thing that was said in the note," said Nina.

"Did you recognize the voice?" he probed.

71

"No, I'd never heard it before," said Nina.

"You don't have a clue, do you?" said Roger.

"No, nothing, and I'm so worried about Annette," pleaded Nina.

He tried not to believe her, but he felt that she was so honest and sincere that what she was saying had to be true.

"You need to go to the police," he said.

"I can't. What if he saw me go to the police? He is liable to kill Annette to protect himself from being found out," Nina explained.

"He's probably going to kill her anyway," Roger said softly.

"He hasn't yet. I can feel it in my bones that she's still alive. But, if I go to the police he may finish the job," she said anxiously.

"Why do you think he hasn't killed her?" he questioned.

"He wouldn't be so worried about me finding her if he had already killed Annette. Can you understand that what I'm saying is just a feeling; a gut feeling? I think she's still alive and needs help," pleaded Nina.

"Do you think he's been following you?" Roger asked as he glanced around the room.

"He has to be, or he wouldn't know where I am. I haven't told a soul at the orphanage," she answered.

"I guess you're right about that. He must be following you. How about having the police come here?" he asked.

"No," she replied. "He's probably got someone guarding the place if he's not doing it himself."

He sat there and stared into space searching for an answer. He couldn't think of anything she could do.

"Maybe someone could take the note to the police for you and tell them what has happened," he suggested.

"That might work," she said as she smiled sweetly at him.

He knew he would have to take the note to the police.

"Don't you have any friends?" he asked.

"No, you're the only person I know."

Now he was really stuck. Now he would have to take the note. He got up to leave.

Nina was so happy she kissed him excitedly, causing her lips to brush against his cheek. She had someone that could help her. He went out of the room on cloud nine. The only thing wrong was she kissed him on the wrong place.

He arrived on the first floor when he remembered that had he forgotten the note. He went back up to five without having exited the elevator on one, where a guest boarded the elevator with him. He walked quickly down the hall and knocked on Nina's door when he heard a muffled cry. It was coming from her room.

"Nina, Nina, open the door!" he shouted as he banged on the locked door with his fist.

Suddenly the door swung open, causing Roger to rush forward nearly losing his footing and fall to the floor. He looked around. No one was to be seen except the startled guest who had exited the elevator with him. He wondered how the door opened by itself. He started to close the door when he saw Nina. She was behind the door lying face down.

"Nina, are you okay?" he said as he gently lifted her and put her on the bed. He noticed that around her neck there were scratches as though someone tried to strangle her.

"Roger, he tried to kill me. A man tried to kill me. I never saw him before," she said as she reached for her throat.

"I'm calling the police now, Nina, and I'm telling them you need an ambulance."

She didn't try to stop him. She let him take over and help her anyway that he could.

Nina's screams and Roger's knocks on Nina's door caused a crowd to gather in the hall. When the police came to her room, they tried to break the crowd up, but not all of the people would leave.

The men from the ambulance put her on the stretcher and took her to the hospital. She looked as though she couldn't breathe, so they gave her some oxygen. Roger showed the police the note when they took him to the police station. They awaited a call from the hospital allowing them to talk to Nina.

"Nina Olson is being stalked and threatened by a person who knows she is searching for her friend. She doesn't know who it is or why it's happening. That's all I can tell you, because that's all I know."

Roger explained the best he could about the note. He told the police exactly what Nina had told him. It wasn't much, but she didn't know very much either. They held him as a suspect for a while and released him when someone verified his statement that he had been in the elevator while all this was happening. He went directly to the hospital to see Nina.

Nina had been hysterical so they gave her a sedative to calm her. That meant more waiting, at least, until she came out from under the sedative. To Roger it seemed as though all he had been doing for his whole life was waiting. Now he had to wait some more. He went back to Nina's room at the motel to look it over. The police had already gone over it, but they might have overlooked something. No such luck. There was nothing there.

He called the doctor at the hospital to see if he could visit Nina, but he said she couldn't be disturbed.

CHAPTER 10

"Harry, is it okay if I go for a ride?" Ann asked.

"Yeah, I guess so, but ride Betsy. She needs the exercise. Don't stay gone too long," Harry answered.

"Okay, I promise to get back early," whispered Ann.

Ann went outside to saddle the horse.

"Where are you going? Not to the mountain, I hope," asked Luke as he entered the barn.

"No, just going for a ride. I'll go in the direction opposite the mountain if that will make you happy," she answered as she displayed a warm smile.

"Well, I'd join you if I could, but I still got some chores to do," he said as he returned her smile with one of his own.

That was close, she thought. She didn't want him to go with her, because she wanted to make those three telephone calls.

It took about a half hour to ride over a hill and through a big field before she got to the pay phone. It was at the gas station, and when the attendant went out to take care of a car, she started to dial the telephone. She decided to call the numbers in alphabetical order. The Florida number would be called first.

She dialed the operator and asked her if it was a long distance number. The operator said it was and told her it was seventy-five cents for three minutes. The operator put her call through to the number with the Florida prefix.

"Hello, Sunnydale Orphanage," said a female voice.

"Hello," she said meekly.

"May I help you?" asked the strange but familiar voice.

"Yes you may. I found a change purse with your telephone number listed inside of it on a small piece of paper. There were two other telephone numbers on that same paper, but I decided to call your number first."

"All right. What can I do for you?"

"I don't know. I don't know who the change purse belongs to, and I need to return the money that I found inside of the purse."

"Oh, I see. Was there much money?"

"Fifty dollars, but I want to return it to its rightful owner. Can you help me?" asked Ann.

"Let me have the other telephone numbers," said the voice.

"Why?" asked Ann.

"I'll call them and see who they belong to. Maybe we can figure out who lost the change purse. It might belong to a former resident at this facility."

Ann was hesitant at first, but she decided it was for the best. She told the voice what the telephone numbers were.

"That would be kind of you. I'm on a pay telephone, and I don't have any more change."

"Let me have the number for the phone that you're calling from and I'll call you back as soon as I place these other two calls. Your voice sounds familiar to me. Have you ever called here before today?"

"No, not that I recall," answered Ann truthfully.

"Tell me your name so I'll know who to ask for," said the voice.

"Ann, err, Ann Patterson. May I ask who you might be?" she asked.

"I'm Mary Boothe. I run the orphanage."

After a quick goodbye, Ann hung up the telephone. She had to tell Mary Boothe her name was Ann Patterson because that was the only one she could remember. Would Mary Boothe really call back and tell her to whom the telephone numbers belonged?

It was getting late, and still there was no call. She waited and waited. To her it seemed like the seconds had turned to months and minutes to years. Finally there it was—a ring. The telephone was ringing. She answered it before the station attendant could get up from where he was sitting.

"Hello," said Mary. "Is that you, Ann?"

"Yes, yes. What did you find out?" asked Ann.

"Well," said Mary. "The Glendale number was for a lawyer, a Mr. Johnson, and the other number was for a studio."

"A studio? What kind of studio?" asked Ann.

"I think it was a movie studio," said Mary. "Yes, now I'm sure. It was a movie studio; the one where Rita Taylor made her last picture."

"Thank you for all your help," said Ann. "How can I ever repay you?"

"That's all right," said Mary. "I enjoyed helping."

Then there was silence. Ann hung up the telephone and looked around. The attendant asked what was wrong, but she didn't answer. She just went running out of there, jumped on the horse and left like a whirlwind.

The attendant was awed. What could anyone say that could scare her so much? The attendant was wrong. Ann wasn't scared, she was happy.

She remembered who she was! She was Rita Taylor's daughter! Her name was Annette Taylor. She had been living at Sunnydale Orphanage practically all of her life, and that fifty dollars she found was her money!

When she got to the house, she went in screaming, "I know who I am! I know who I am!"

Everyone came running. They looked at Ann who was crying, and yet she was laughing at the same time. When she stopped to get her breath, they asked her what was wrong.

"Nothing, nothing at all," she replied. "It's just that I found out who I am."

"You what?" asked Luke.

"I remember who I am! I'm Annette Taylor."

"That doesn't help much. So you're Annette Taylor. Do you remember where you live?" asked Luke.

"Yes, before I came here I had been living in an orphanage. My parents put me there because they didn't want me to be bothered by reporters for fan magazines. See, my mother was Rita Taylor," she added joyfully. "And my birthday was a few days ago! I just turned seventeen!"

"You can't be!" exclaimed Emma. "She never had no daughter."

"That's what you think," said Ann. "Nobody knew Rita Taylor had a daughter except our lawyer. I'm supposed to inherit everything in Mom and Dad's will."

"But that doesn't explain why anyone would want to kill you," said Granny.

Granny was sorry she had brought the subject up. Everybody just wanted to forget about it.

"Don't you see?" asked Ann. "The lawyer will inherit it if I don't. It says so in the will."

"Don't be silly, child. You're probably just making that story up," said an annoyed Harry.

"No, Pa. Maybe she's right. She could be. After all, do you remember that thing that we found? There was a locket with a picture of Rita Taylor in it," said Luke as he was getting interested in what she said. Luke would believe anything she said. He loved her too much to do otherwise. Ann was relieved. At least someone believed her.

"All of you listen to me," said Ann. "I want you to go over to the gas station and make a telephone call. I want you to call the Sunnydale Orphanage and ask for Annette Taylor's description."

They looked at each other and then at Ann. At first no one but Luke wanted to go, but her pleading eyes made their decision for them. They all piled into the car. They would have gone in the wagon, but Granny said she didn't want to be bounced around so much.

It didn't take them very long to get there. They stopped in front of the gas tanks and asked the attendant to fill it up. No one said much. The silence was probably because no one wanted to get his or her hopes up and then have them dashed back down to the ground by the truth.

Ann jumped out and ran to the telephone. Harry got some money out of his pocket while Ann got the number. At first she thought she lost the paper, but she soon found it in her pocket.

Luke was holding her hand while Harry started dialing. Luke looked at Ann affectionately. She pulled her hand from his. Everyone was watching the telephone as if it was something special. The telephone rang twice on the other end of the line.

"Hello," said Mary.

"Howdy," said Harry. "I was just inquiring about a description of Annette Taylor. There is a girl that has been staying with us. Granny said she has am...er...amnesia. She's been with us quite a while. She just recollected who she was today."

"Well, I'm not supposed to tell other people, but I know Annette Taylor has been gone from the orphanage for about a month. I can tell you from memory," said Mary.

"All right, ma'am, tell me," said Harry.

"Her hair is brown. She has brown eyes and a light complexion," said Mary.

"Is there anything else unique that you can tell me about her?" he asked.

"She is not very tall. She is seventeen years old. And, oh yeah, she has a small heart-shaped birthmark on the back of her neck," replied the orphanage supervisor.

"Thank you," Harry said, and he hung up the telephone.

He looked at Ann. The description fit perfectly. He had seen the birthmark on her neck. He stood there a few moments with his mouth open. Emma nudged him, and he told them what Mary had said. A frown came to Luke's face.

"What's wrong?" asked Ann.

Luke didn't say anything. He started walking, and he didn't turn around when his father called him. Ann was worried. She didn't know what was wrong with him. She wanted him to be happy for her.

"Harry, why don't you, Granny and Emma go back to the house without me? I want to walk home with Luke," Ann said. She had to run a little before catching up with him.

"Luke, Luke, what's wrong?" she pleaded tugging on his arm.

He didn't say anything but kept on walking. He was heading for the shortcut. When he reached the edge of the woods, he sat down. Ann sat down beside him and asked again, "What's wrong, Luke?"

"Well, I'll tell you," said Luke. "You being famous and all, you will probably go to California and live. I...or we...will never see you again."

She smiled because she knew what was wrong. "Luke, I'll see you quite a lot after I'm eighteen."

"What do you mean?" asked confused Luke.

"Well, eighteen doesn't sound too young to get married does it? Seventeen, I believe, is too young," she said looking at him, hoping he would catch the gigantic hint.

"You mean you will marry me?" asked Luke very much surprised.

80

"If you want me, but remember, not until after my next birthday," she said.

He was about to kiss her when a shot rang out from nowhere. Luke pulled her to the ground to get her out of the way when he was hit.

"Luke, you need help really fast. You're bleeding a lot," she said as she tried to stop the blood flow with her hand.

Ann didn't know what to do. She couldn't carry him. He was too big. She started running to the road when she heard a gun being cocked. Whoever shot him was after her now. She was frantic. She could run, but he could still shoot at her and maybe even hit her.

She started running. She ran as noiselessly as possible, but whoever was after her was getting closer. She saw an old cave. Her mind flashed back to her nightmare where she couldn't get out of the dark cave. There was no reason on Earth that could make her go inside that cave. There would be no way out of it, not for her. Her unconscious dreams had told her that bit of information. If she went inside, he was sure to kill her, so she tried to climb above it. She had made it behind a rock when he came carefully approaching the cave. He went inside for a few seconds, came back out and went in again.

Ann was starting to move when a small rock rolled down to the foot of the cave. He heard it and came out of the cave immediately. He looked toward the direction from where the rock had rolled and swung the gun through the air menacingly.

Ann saw him and started running again. She ran as fast as she could, but she didn't seem to go anywhere. On and on she went. She paused for a second to see if he was still behind her. She heard him and started running again. She was completely exhausted. She couldn't go any further. She slumped to the ground and made no movement. She knew he would probably kill her.

He came on running. She wanted to scream at him and ask him why he was trying to kill her. She didn't know this man. Was he working for someone who would pay him to kill Annette Taylor? She knew who would dole out the blood money. It had to be the man who would inherit it if she was dead. Would he have gone so far as to kill her mother and father?

He got within a few feet of her and was about to pull the trigger when someone jumped him from behind. Ann couldn't believe her eyes. Luke was fighting the man. Luke, with a bullet a few inches from his heart was fighting to protect her. She jumped to her feet and went after the gun. It had fallen to the ground during the scuffle. When she reached it, she picked it up and pointed it at the two men fighting.

The stranger pushed Luke to the ground, and Ann pointed the gun straight at his head. She told him to put his hands up.

"I'll shoot your head off, Mister, if you don't do what I tell you to do!" she screamed as she fought to maintain control of the shaking gun.

At first he thought he could get the gun away from her. He started to move toward her, but when he saw her eyes, he knew he couldn't. She was very much determined to keep it.

"Put that gun down, little lady, before you hurt yourself," he said.

"The only one who is going to get hurt around is you, Mister. You shot Luke, so now you're going to have to help him. Get him up on his feet and start walking toward the road. Do it now, Mister!" said Ann in a stern forceful tone, meaning anything and everything she said.

It was very painful for Luke, but he had to go. She couldn't leave him behind.

They walked and walked. They didn't think they were ever going to see the road.

Finally, there it was. Only it was deserted. Not a single car was on it.

"Sit down and don't you be moving except to help Luke," said Ann, the gun still clenched tightly in her hands.

The stranger did as he was told. He didn't want to rile Ann any more than was necessary. She was nervous, and her finger was actively caressing the trigger of the gun. The stranger laid Luke down on the ground. Ann went over to see what she could do to help him.

The wound looked as though it was angry and red as blood continued to trickle. The bullet had to come out—fast.

She went to the stranger and told him to empty his pockets. He had six more bullets in his pockets. She removed Luke's belt and her own belt to use them to tie the stranger's hands and feet.

The only way to get people to hear her was to shoot. She shot in the air twice. Hopefully someone would hear the shots and come to see what was wrong.

She waited about an hour, but still no one came.

The stranger had a cigarette lighter, so she took it and started a fire. She took Luke's knife from his pocket and held it over the fire. She was going to take the bullet out. If she didn't, he would die. She surely didn't want that to happen.

She got the germs off the knife by holding it over the fire and walked over to Luke. He was conscious and knew what she was going to do, but didn't say anything to stop her. She stuffed her handkerchief in his mouth, so he could bite into it.

She tore his shirt away from the wound and started probing for the bullet. It was very painful for him, but he didn't cry out. A moan was all he emitted before he thankfully passed out and removed himself from the pain.

She tore the bottom part of her shirt off to stop his wound from bleeding. She sat there watching him a little longer. She heard something coming.

"A car," said as she jumped up. "There is car coming!" She grabbed the gun and ran.

"Stop! Stop! Please help me!" she screamed.

The car pulled to a stop. The driver jumped out to see what was wrong. She led him to Luke.

"He tried to kill me, but he missed me and hit him," she said as she pointed to the stranger whom she had tied up the best she could with the belts. The driver didn't know what to do, but if he didn't help Luke he knew that Luke would soon die.

"Help me get him into the car," he told Ann. "And I'll take him to the hospital and then drop you two off at the sheriff's office."

Ann helped the driver load Luke into the car, then she forced the stranger to walk to the car at gunpoint after she loosened his legs from the belt.

It didn't take very long to get Luke to the hospital. After a few words of explanation, Ann and the hand-bound stranger were being escorted to the sheriff's office by a reluctant good samaritan.

When Ann went inside the sheriff's office, she walked behind the stranger with his hands bound up by a belt behind his back. The deputies didn't know what to think. Some of them even laughed at the sight of a small girl like her overpowering a large man like him.

Ann and the stranger were both held in custody until Luke could talk. They interrogated the man and found out his name. It was Don Wilson. He was working for a lawyer named Arthur Johnson.

"Arthur Johnson!" exclaimed Ann. "He was the lawyer who worked for my mother and father."

CHAPTER 11

"Do you know the man who attacked you?" asked a deputy sheriff as he probed for answers.

"No, I've never seen him before," answered Nina.

"What did he look like?" continued the deputy.

"He was about six feet tall and heavy set. He wasn't fat, but he was big," said Nina.

"What was he wearing?" probed the deputy.

"I don't remember. Blue jeans I think and some kind of plaid shirt," she said as if she were searching her mind.

"How about his eyes? What color were they?" the deputy continued.

"Brown, they were brown and mean-looking," said Nina as she closed her eyes trying to think.

"What about his skin?" said the deputy.

"He was fair," she responded.

"Do you remember anything else about him?" he asked.

"No, except that he was strong," she answered softly.

When the deputy left, Roger tried to console her. Nina was feeling better after a couple of hours; well enough to get up and continue her search.

"Roger, tell them I want to leave," Nina said.

"What's the hurry?" he asked.

"I'm getting close. Annette's really close and very much alive. I need to find her," Nina explained.

"I don't want you leaving here alone. I'll go with you," he told her.

"You don't have to do that. You've already done so much," she said softly.

"Yes, Nina, I have to help you. I love you. I can't help myself," Roger said as he smiled.

Nina wrapped her arms around Roger and kissed him directly on the mouth, not the cheek. He returned her kiss long enough to let her know that he was with her in whatever decision she made.

Nina and Roger left the hospital. The first thing Nina did was go directly to the sheriff's office and ask if anything had been reported to them about Annette.

"Deputy," she said timidly. "I'm inquiring about a girl named Annette Taylor. She's been missing for quite a while, and I have been looking for her. She is my best friend. Have you heard anything about her?"

The deputy said he would have to look at the records to find out. Nina sat down on one of the chairs against the wall to wait.

"Miss, oh, miss," said the deputy. "This report says she has been living on a farm outside of town. Someone had tried to shoot her boyfriend, or I should say someone shot her boyfriend. She brought the person in who did it. He tried to kill her, too."

Nina was terrified. She and Roger ran out to the car and started for the farm after getting directions from the deputy. Why would anyone want to harm her? It didn't take them long to drive to the farm, and when she arrived at the farmhouse Nina was afraid to go inside. She didn't know why she was afraid except that she didn't want to be disappointed. She had been looking and worrying for so long that she didn't know if she could stand another disappointment.

Nina stayed in the car and Roger knocked on the door. Emma answered the door and asked him what he wanted.

"Is a Miss Annette Taylor here?" he asked.

"Oh, you mean Ann. Step inside, and I'll see," she said as she pointed at the place to sit down.

Emma went through the house yelling for Ann. When Ann entered the room he asked, "Do you know a Nina Olson?"

"Yes, yes, do you know where she is? Is she all right?" asked Ann.

Roger went to the door and motioned to Nina to come in. Nina came running. When she saw Annette, she screamed with joy and embraced her.

"Why didn't you write?" asked Nina.

"I couldn't," replied Ann. "I didn't know who I was."

Ann noticed how pale Nina looked.

"Sit down," she said. "You look ill."

"I am," Nina said. "Someone tried to keep me from looking for you."

"Do you know what he looked like?" asked Ann very much interested in what Nina had to say.

"Yes, he had brown hair and brown eyes. He was heavy set with a fair complexion."

"That was who I thought it was," said Ann. "He was Mom and Dad's lawyer."

They went back to the sheriff's office together and told them who it was that had attacked Nina. The sheriff said he would put out an all-points bulletin and have Nina's attacker picked up.

When Arthur Johnson was arrested at a routine traffic stop, he admitted everything. He denied that he had anything to do with the death of Rita Taylor and her husband. He claimed that just happened without any help from him. He never thought of doing away with Annette Taylor until after the death of her parents. He said if she was dead, he would collect the inheritance.

There were millions of dollars up for grabs and Arthur wanted it all. He didn't want it to go into the hands of a teenager. He had worked too hard and too long to lose his grip on that money. He said he had debts to pay, big debts that had to be paid, no matter what.

As long as Annette Taylor didn't know who she was, he wasn't too worried about her. He knew he would have to deal with her eventually, but she wasn't a pressing problem.

Nina Olson became Arthur's problem. She was the one who was giving him fits. He had to discourage her any way he could, even if he had to kill her. The police made a determination that Ann's parents were killed in an accident. It didn't appear that they were murdered.

Roger and Nina were inseparable. They stayed at Roger's motel close to the Hamiltons and were always around to help Ann and Luke. After the case was closed, Roger and Nina were going to get married.

It wasn't the same for Ann, though. She wasn't eighteen. Luke was in the hospital, and she had to go to California to take care of the inheritance.

She and Luke had made a sacred promise. When Annette, or Ann as she preferred to be called, celebrated her eighteenth birthday, they would get married.

She would be "Mrs. Luke Hamilton" and proud of it. She planned to share her wealth with the Hamilton family for all of the kindness they had offered her when she needed it most.

EPILOGUE

A year passed and Annette Taylor returned to stay with her new family in their newly built home paid for with money inherited from the estate of her mother and father.

She would live in the mountains of Virginia where she planned to marry Luke and start a family of their own.

She was known to them as Ann, and that was what she wanted to be called. Ann was the young lady who was loved as a stray walking in from the mountains.

Ann always wanted to remember how welcomed she felt with her new family. They could have easily cast her aside and told her to fend for herself. But not the Hamiltons, they were not that kind of people.

Ann would forever be grateful that she had been found by Luke and was claimed as family, and within no time that would be made legal when Ann would take the marriage vows that would legally give her the name of Mrs. Luke Hamilton.

About the Author

Linda Hudson Hoagland of Tazewell, Virginia, graduate of Southwest Virginia Community College, has won acclaim for her novels, short stories, essays and poems. Many of her works have been published in anthologies such as *Cup of Comfort* along with the publication of her five mystery novels, six nonfiction books, a short story collection and young adult novel.

A few of the awards won by Linda Hudson Hoagland are as follows:

2012 – Dream Quest One – First Place – Short Story – "I Am Mom"

2012 – Alabama Writers Conclave – Honorable Mention – Traditional Poem – "A Dream Trip"

2012 – Westmoreland Arts & Heritage Festival – Honorable Mention – Short Story – "Welcome to Whistler"

2012 – Virginia Writers Club – Second Place – Nonfiction – "No Service"

2012 – West Virginia Writers – Honorable Mention – Stage Play – *I'm Not Ready*

2012 – The Seacoast Writers Association – Third Place – Nonfiction – *Getting Myself Primed*

2012 – Tennessee Mountain Writers – Second Place – Fiction – "And the Next Day"

2012 – Women's Memoirs – All Things Labor – Honorable Mention – "Penance"

2011 – Alabama Writers Conclave – Honorable Mention – First Chapter of a Novel– "Writing the Circuit"

2011 – Alabama Writers Conclave – Second Prize – Juvenile Fiction – "The Lady in the Sun"

2011 – Appalachian Heritage Writers Symposium – Second Place – Adult Essay – "Surprise Package"

2011 – Writers-Editors Network International Writing Competition – Honorable Mention – Nonfiction – "Getting Myself Primed"

2011 – Tennessee Mountain Writers – Third Place – Writing for Young People – "I Dare You"

2010 – The Jesse Stuart Prize for Young Adult Writing – Second Place – "How's That For Real"

2010 – Tampa Writers Alliance – Novel – Honorable Mention – "Quilt Pieces"

2010 – Alabama Writers Conclave – Nonfiction – Third Prize – "Four Large Eggs"

2008 – Nominee Governor's Award for the Arts

2007 – Sherwood Anderson Short Story Contest – First Place – "Category V"

Many other awards have not been listed.

If you liked
THE BEST DARN SECRET,
check out these books by
LITTLE CREEK BOOKS authors
Rebecca Williams Spindler and her
teenage daughter, Madelyn Spindler!

The Tale of Two Sisters

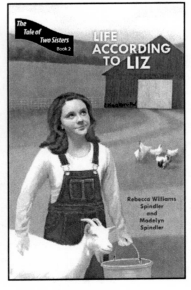

Jan-Carol Publishing, Inc

Mountain Girl Press

LITTLE CREEK BOOKS

Books for discerning readers

www.jancarolpublishing.com

www.facebook.com/MountainGirlPress
www.facebook.com/LittleCreekBooks

CPSIA information can be obtained at www.ICGtesting.com
Printed in the USA
BVOW081145251012

303881BV00001B/2/P

9 781939 289001